I0630889

A VENGEFUL
Affair

A VENGEFUL
Affair

CARMEN
FALCONE

This book is a work of fiction. Names, characters, places, and incidents
are the product of the author's imagination or are used fictitiously.
Any resemblance to actual events, locales, or persons, living or dead, is
coincidental.

Copyright © 2015 by Carmen Falcone. All rights reserved, including the
right to reproduce, distribute, or transmit in any form or by any means.
For information regarding subsidiary rights, please contact the Publisher.

Entangled Publishing, LLC
10940 S Parker Rd
Suite 327
Parker, CO 80134
rights@entangledpublishing.com

Indulgence is an imprint of Entangled Publishing, LLC.

Edited by Ruth Homrighaus
Cover design by LJ Anderson/Mayhem Cover Creations
Cover art from kupicoo/iStock

Manufactured in the United States of America

First Edition July 2012

To Gian, my supportive and long-suffering husband.

*You make the hard times shorter and
the good times longer.*

Chapter One

Almost there.

Vivian Foster took a deep breath and wrapped her fingers around the door handle, the steel a cold weight in her palm. The key was already inside the lock, and she knew the moment she opencd that door, everything she'd been taught by her parents would disappear.

Be good. Do the right thing. Don't steal.

Her conscience justified her action. *Stealing is okay if it fixes a bigger wrong.*

Revenge had its own moral code.

This was not the time for moral dilemmas. If she wanted to search Javier Rivera's office before the security team made its nightly rounds, she had to stop thinking about what she was about to do. Javier needed to pay for killing Molly, and Vivian knew just the price—his coveted billion-pound merger.

It had been naive of Molly to start an office affair with the boss, but she hadn't deserved to be fired for it, and she'd done nothing to deserve the emotional abuse that followed. And when Molly had retaliated by trying to take Rivera's precious merger from him, he'd had her followed and harassed. Within a week of having her flat vandalized, Molly had been found dead in her bedroom. All alone.

The police had ruled it a suicide, but Vivian knew her friend would never shoot herself. Javier had done it—or ordered it done.

He killed her. Don't forget. You heard his voice mail.

She entered the room, relocked the door, and withdrew the key. Slipping it into her pocket, she shut the door again with a small click. Vivian used a sleek flashlight to guide her through the spacious, dark office. She didn't want to draw any attention by turning the overhead lights on.

Floor-to-ceiling glass along one wall showcased the twinkling lights along the opposite bank of the river Thames. Her white beam skipped over a long leather sofa, a low glass coffee table scattered with business magazines and international newspapers, a trio of bookshelves, a sleek refrigerator and minibar, then finally to the desk.

Vivian's grasp on the flashlight loosened for a moment as cold sweat slicked her palm. Since her position was at the reception desk, she'd never been to the CEO's office before. Mrs. Wright, his snooty personal assistant, screened all of his calls and appointments.

She walked among the shadows that stretched along the polished hardwood floor, approaching the heavy glass-and-metal desk, which had probably been custom made. Money was all that mattered to a man like Javier Rivera.

For a moment, she considered the computer in front of her, then shook her head, knowing the network would be secure. Sitting on the edge of the soft leather chair, she flashed her light over the desktop. Her fingers tapped the metal drawers, and she tried to pull them open with no luck. Contracts, notes, reports…anything would help.

She leaned over the trash bin.

Empty.

So was the recycling bin and the paper shredder.

Vivian had never thought this would be easy, but she had counted on finding *something.* Any piece of information that would lead her to—

Her eyes caught on the edge of a manila folder peeking out from between two finance books. She grabbed it and shone the flashlight on the few pages inside. A report.

She blinked at the numbers, and her breath caught. Could that be…?

Footsteps echoed from outside the door.

Vivian leaped to her feet with a start, her quickened pulse carrying a surge of fear through her and making her painfully alert.

The footsteps came closer. She tucked the folder inside her bag, her gaze riveted to the door.

It could be security. But their rounds weren't supposed to start for another half hour.

There was no time. Vivian picked up the flashlight with unsteady fingers and panned it around the office, looking for a place to hide.

Her first option was a walk-in closet with gray french doors. As the steps slowed outside the office door, she cut across to the closet, slipped inside, and turned off the flashlight.

Squeezed in among hanging suits and leather shoes, she inhaled the pine scent of floor cleaner. At six feet tall, Vivian had always felt out of place, particularly between her petite mother and short stepfather. Now there was no doubt: she wished she were shorter.

A razor of light stabbed through the gap between the closet doors.

Vivian covered her mouth with her hand, holding her breath. She couldn't believe this was happening. Her heart drummed in her ears.

"Tell the pilot to wait. I have to pick up my briefcase." The voice was deep, with a strong Spanish accent.

Vivian blinked, swallowing the lump in her throat. This wasn't security. This was Javier Rivera.

She'd seen him cross the reception area quite a few times, always talking on his mobile. He'd never greeted her with more than a nod, but she'd heard his commanding voice as he spoke to others. And now he was within feet of her, and she was hiding among his Italian suits.

Vivian stiffened. His footsteps approached her hiding place. She closed her eyes and hoped he would just turn around and go away.

Silence.

His footfalls faded, and she let her breath out in small gasps, desperation almost turning her into an optimist.

His briefcase could be anywhere in his office, couldn't it? Nowhere obvious, or she'd have spotted it. The odds were that Javier Rivera would simply leave to get on his private jet, and she'd still have time to resume her search in his office and then vanish before the security team returned.

The doors swung open. Bright light filled her hiding place.

Vivian blinked.

Up close, Javier Rivera looked a lot more intimidating. His rugged face was framed by short, dark-brown hair. He had a slight bump on his otherwise aristocratic nose and a small scar on his chin. He was several inches taller than her, broad-shouldered and powerful.

She opened her mouth to speak, but no sound came out.

Javier's angry black eyes locked with hers, and she stood completely still, frozen like a winter river. Her heart galloped.

"What the hell are you doing in here?" he asked.

Vivian swallowed. "M–Mr. Rivera. I'm so sorry. I came to deliver a fax, and when I heard someone coming in, I got scared and hid in the closet." Vivian stepped out of her hiding place and tried to push past him, but Javier didn't give an inch.

He studied her face, his full lips tight and a glint of disbelief in his eyes.

"I was on my way out when these came." Vivian's fingers trembled as she opened her messenger bag and handed him a couple of sheets of paper she'd brought along in the event she needed a cover story. "Since Mrs. Wright had already gone home, I wanted to hand-deliver these. They're marked 'confidential.'"

Javier's eyes scanned the pages. "All faxes that come to me say 'confidential.' These are only confirmations of dinner reservations and hotel arrangements."

"Well, sir, there they are." She managed a smile, holding the strap of her bag so tightly her knuckles whitened.

For a moment, his eyes trailed down her neckline. Was he staring at her chest? Vivian crossed her arms, and Javier pointed to the place where her name tag should have been.

"What's your name?" he demanded.

"Vivian Foster, sir." She squared her shoulders.

"How did you get in, Ms. Foster?"

"I used the master key."

He frowned. "You shouldn't have access to it."

"Look, Mr. Rivera, I'm sorry about this misunderstanding. I wanted to drop these off because I thought they were important." Vivian shook her head. "I didn't even know what they were about. I'm new here…"

She glanced around the office. It had a cool sophistication that unsettled her. Or perhaps it was the man who did that. The black leather sofas, contemporary standing lamps, and Surrealist art had nothing on Javier's inquisitive posture, his eyes piercing through hers, and his mocking smile.

"How convenient for you to be at my office after hours," Javier said drily. "Are you looking for a shortcut up the corporate ladder, Ms. Foster? Since you are *new*?"

"A shortcut?" Vivian's eyes narrowed. "I'm offended you would think I need to cheat to move up any ladder." She raised her chin and tried again to move past him. "I'll go, and I'll pretend you didn't say that, Mr. Rivera."

"Not so fast, Ms. Foster." He seized her wrist, his unwelcome touch sending a shiver through her body.

He was so massive, his nearness almost made her feel delicate, which she knew she was not. "But sir…" She tried to twist from his grasp. He carefully turned her to face him, reducing the gap between them and holding her captive with those dark eyes.

A murderer's eyes. She'd had six months since Molly's death to learn to hate him.

Javier leaned over her, his hot breath fanning her earlobe. "Ms. Foster, I will ask you one more time. What were you doing in here?"

She breathed in deeply, trying to regain control, but succeeded only in inhaling the minty scent of his aftershave.

"Mr. Rivera, I already…" She gasped when he patted her shoulders, then ran his hands down and around to brush the sides of her breasts.

"How dare you—" Vivian choked on her words, angry that he would touch her so blatantly.

"I'm making sure you don't have any weapons," Javier said casually, as if touching a woman he barely knew was the most natural thing in the world.

Well, for him it probably is.

He brushed his hands over her stomach and hips. His brief touch was neither sexual nor aggressive, yet the weight of his long fingers on her black polyester suit made her blood pound hotly through her veins. His hands moved down her long legs, and she avoided looking directly at him when he knelt down, touching the hem of her pants and sliding his fingers softly along the inside of her ankles.

"No weapons." Vivian raised her voice, yanking away from his touch. Javier Rivera had no right to—

He slid her bag off her shoulder and abruptly upended it over his desk.

"You can't do that!" Vivian said, feeling a wave of heat rising to stain her cheeks. He had just played her for a fool. She should have known. Nothing Javier did was pointless.

"You aren't looking for a promotion," he said calmly. He picked up the folder she'd found, a pack of gum, her mobile, a small wallet, and a makeup case. Stray coins rolled along the desk and fell to the floor.

Vivian took a deep breath as she bent to collect the coins, picking them off the hardwood to escape the inquisition of his eyes. "Of course I'm not."

When she rose to her feet, smoothing her ponytail with one hand and clenching the cold coins with the other, he glared at her, his arms folded.

"What was my folder doing in your bag?"

"Your folder?" She frowned. "I was about to place your fax on your desk when I heard a noise, and I pushed them into my bag. I must have picked up the folder at the same time." Vivian wondered how much longer she'd have to lie. It was new to her, and dodging his questions made her feel like a circus juggler. A first-day-on-the-job circus juggler. All the balls could drop at any time.

"Ms. Foster, I am not patient or stupid. You came in when I wasn't supposed to be here. When *no one* was supposed to be here. And you have in your possession confidential information of a business transaction which I had left on my desk."

"I didn't even know what that was," Vivian said innocently.

He opened the side zipper of her messenger bag and rummaged around with long, tanned fingers. "Planning on going somewhere?" Javier held her passport up.

"That's none of your business."

"Ms. Foster, do you really want to make things harder for yourself?"

"I'm going to South America with friends in a few months. I brought my passport to make copies of it. I'm applying for a visa, though it's really none of your business."

"You have an answer for everything, don't you, Ms. Foster?" Javier examined her driver's license, his eyes narrowing over the picture.

"Give me back my things." She reached for her bag, then scooped her makeup case, wallet, and other personal items inside. "Mr. Rivera, I need my passport and my mobile. If you don't give them to me right now—" She stretched her open hand toward him, but he pocketed both items.

"Yes, go on. What will you do, Ms. Foster?" His lips curved into a cynical smile. "Call the police?"

Vivian clenched her fists, her short fingernails digging hard into her palms. "I should, shouldn't I? After being harassed as if I'm some lowlife burglar by the CEO."

"Yes, I can make that call myself. But I guarantee you the outcome won't be favorable to you. What were you looking for?" There it was, that predatory look again, assessing her from top to bottom.

"But I already said—"

"Whoever is paying you, I can pay you double if you cooperate."

"It's all about money to you, isn't it?" Vivian looked deep into his black eyes, where pure challenge flickered. She held his gaze, refusing to back down.

She was here to be the instrument of Molly's revenge. All the money in the world couldn't turn her away from that goal.

To her relief, Javier's phone rang. He gestured to her to stay put and took his call just outside his office, leaving the heavy door open.

Vivian watched him at first, unable to hear, then gave up and began pacing the floor. After a while, the sound of her shoes scraping over the hardwood irritated her, and she sat down to pray for a miracle.

"She stole the Webb proposal," his solicitor repeated on the other end of the line.

"Yes." Javier paced the floor of the waiting area adjoining his office.

"You may call the police, although they won't hold her for long. The publicity won't be good for the Broussard merger, either."

"*Infierno!* This is the worst timing." Javier ran his hand through his hair.

"Yes, Monsieur Broussard is known for being volatile. If you take her to the police, the press will know, and he will know. It was hard enough hiding what happened to that other woman."

Molly. He'd made a mistake there, broken one of his cardinal rules, and he'd paid for it many times over. How foolish of him to think the matter had ended with the woman's death. "Molly Richardson was irrational. I wonder if Vivian works for the same people?"

"If she goes to jail, we may never know. Whoever hired her may back off or think of a different approach."

"I've worked the last year nonstop for this merger to happen. I can't lose it now."

I've waited for this moment my whole life.

Javier stopped pacing and looked across at the woman who had disrupted his evening in more ways than one. She was sitting elegantly, her legs crossed at the ankles. Collected and goal-oriented, she appeared nothing like the irrational, impulsive Molly Richardson.

"I won't lose it," he continued firmly. "Call Matt Smith, the private investigator, and have him find out what he can about Vivian Foster."

"And what will you do in the meantime?"

"I will take Ms. Foster out of commission while we check her credentials. Whoever hired her won't find her until I sign my contract."

"But you have to go to Paris tonight."

Javier knew that. If he made big changes to his plans, his opponent might seize the opportunity to destroy the merger. Broussard was in Paris, which meant Javier had to be there as well. If he stuck to his plans and made sure Vivian was unreachable, perhaps he could throw his opponent off.

Until his investigator told him everything he needed to know about Vivian Foster, he would keep her close.

"I'll just have some excess luggage." Javier hung up the phone.

What a night. He'd thought stopping by the office to get his briefcase before heading to Paris was enough of an inconvenience, especially for a man like him, who hated when things went out of control. But then he'd found the new receptionist in his closet, her deep blue eyes startled and her cheeks flushed.

A different kind of inconvenience altogether.

Javier had noticed her a few times, but he would never have imagined the stern receptionist as a threat to his company. While the other women at the front desk smiled in welcome as he passed them, Vivian would simply nod an acknowledgment and return to answering the phones or checking something on her computer screen.

He slid the phone into his pocket and returned to his office silently, observing the beautiful woman sitting before him. There was a veneer of vulnerability about her when she didn't know she was being watched. When she wasn't trying so hard to clash with him.

If the circumstances were different…

He could think of a pleasurable way to make her talk, and moan. He would take that silly ponytail apart and run his fingers through her dark auburn hair. He'd kiss those rosy lips until they swelled, slide his mouth down her neck as he inhaled the fresh lavender fragrance she wore. The same fragrance that had caught his attention and prompted him to open his closet doors.

And he would outline her curves with his bare hands, a much more intimate exploration than his impersonal frisking.

His eyes moved to the outline of her full breasts, the indentation of her waist…and those long, long legs lost inside a shapeless pair of pants.

Basta! He cleared his throat. A few months without sex could really compromise a man's common sense.

Vivian Foster was an industrial spy. She was the last woman he ought to be wasting his time fantasizing about.

In a few days, he would make his imprint on the global market forever and not only surpass his stepfather's wealth but prove that he'd made it all on his own.

Nobody would stop him. Certainly not Ms. Foster, with her sparkling blue eyes.

Discovering the identity of his real enemy was paramount. Vivian Foster was not the one who was trying to ruin him, but if he played his cards right, she could take him to the man who was—whether she wanted to or not.

"Mr. Rivera, can I please go now?" Vivian got to her feet the moment her eyes found his. He smiled inside, recognizing that her defenses were on full alert.

"How did you get the master key?"

"There was an old copy in the manager's box. This is the first time I've used it, and believe me, it will be the last. I went out of my way to please you, and yet you have completely misread me."

Javier took a deep breath, desperate to remove from his mind the image of the guarded woman in front of him going out of her way to please him. "Today is Friday. It didn't occur to you to drop the faxes in Mrs. Wright's box?"

"No, Mr. Rivera. You work on weekends, and I thought it might have been urgent."

"Why did you hide when I walked in?"

"Because I was a woman alone in an empty office building at night."

"Ms. Foster, I have no time to waste. My private jet is waiting for me, and I'm expected in Paris for the weekend."

"Well, sir, you should go." Vivian gave him a dismissive shrug and tried to brush past him.

"I intend to. But having to call the police to question you would delay me." He reached out and grabbed her arm to stop her from leaving. "You are not authorized to be in my office. You had something of mine in your bag, and you had your passport with you as though you were planning to leave the country."

"So?"

"My solicitors can give you quite a headache if I want them to. We will talk to security, look through the security tapes, dig into your background, and look for witnesses to your trespassing and theft. But I prefer to avoid that fuss. That's why you are coming with me."

"What? What kind of crazy idea is that?" She widened her eyes. "No."

"Yes. We are leaving for Paris in an hour. I have important business to attend, and you will accompany me."

"But I'm a receptionist. Traveling with the CEO isn't part of my job." Her cheeks flushed again as she protested.

Damn. This woman is good. She can even summon a blush

on command.

"Neither is snooping around my office. Yet here we are."

"But Mr. Rivera, I already explained—"

"No, you have not explained. Not the part that matters. But you will." Javier glanced at his watch. They had to leave soon. He took his briefcase from the file drawer in the credenza located behind the black leather sofa. "Either you come with me so I can ask you a few questions in private, or I call the police and my solicitors, and they take care of you."

"You wouldn't." Panic flared in her enormous blue eyes.

"Try me." He waved his phone. "No time. Yes or no?" Javier flipped the lights off.

"For how long?"

"Only enough time for me to make sure you are who you say you are, Ms. Foster."

"I can't believe this," she muttered under her breath.

"And I can't believe you. But if you are innocent, you shouldn't be afraid." Javier looked at the shadow of uncertainty in her eyes, the one she was obviously trying so hard to hide.

Who was she working for? And why? Was it only money that motivated her, or was she helping a lover?

Yes, that made sense… Only a woman blinded by passion would put her freedom, job, and dignity at risk.

That was why he stayed away from emotional relationships. He was a passionate man—in his work life, in the bedroom with a beautiful woman in his arms. But he was also a strategist who made sure never to confuse lust with love. He had no time for love, no patience for passion that overpowered common sense.

"Can I have a few minutes to think about this?" Vivian cleared her throat nervously.

"This isn't a car sale, Ms. Foster." Javier glanced at his watch. "But since I'm a generous man, I'll give you one minute."

Chapter Two

A minute! Vivian wanted to scream. Instead, she chewed on her lower lip and held her ground, though her knees threatened to give out at any moment.

If you are innocent, you shouldn't be afraid.

She wasn't innocent, and by the suspicion flashing in his eyes, he knew it. But there was no evidence yet. If she stayed and he called the police and his lawyers, if they went through the security tapes, how long would it take him to link her to Molly?

Not long.

"Thirty seconds," Javier said.

What if she went with him?

At this point, really, there was no better option. She could buy time to call Roger, the man who had helped her get the reception job. The man who wanted to destroy Javier as badly as she did. Maybe he knew something about this trip to Paris. After all, didn't Monsieur Broussard live in Paris?

Vivian folded her arms. It was no coincidence that Javier was on his way to Paris just before the merger signing.

Wouldn't it be easier for her to get the inside scoop if she were close to Javier, rather than far away? He would question her, but maybe she would also be able to find time to do some searching of her own. She would be close to his briefcase, his laptop—not to mention the people around him, who might include employees from the merger team.

If he tried to hurt her in any way, she would be the one reporting him to the police, and he would get what he deserved.

"Fine." Realizing she'd mumbled, she spoke more loudly. "I'll go with you."

Her stomach curled in a tight knot as Javier's lips formed a slow, triumphant smile.

She sat silently during the ride from the office to a private airfield. They boarded his luxurious jet, which had a cabin that was larger and more comfortable than her own bedroom. But Vivian didn't waste much time appreciating the oversized reclining chairs, the built-in rosewood shelves filled with magazines, or the state-of-the-art entertainment center.

She pretended to read the first magazine she picked up, stealing the occasional glance at Javier. He sat opposite her, which she thought was odd, as there were other seats he could have occupied.

Vivian broke the silence. "You still haven't told me how long I'll be away. You didn't let me go home to pick up my clothes."

Javier had been typing mercilessly on the keyboard of his thin laptop. When she spoke, he paused and raised his eyes from the device to her, but he didn't say a word.

"I just thought I needed my things—"

"For the next few days, I will take care of whatever you

need." Javier's accent seemed thicker than usual, and she wondered if she'd somehow angered him.

He returned his attention to the laptop.

Vivian crossed her arms. For the rest of the flight, they didn't exchange a word. She assumed it was because he didn't want to talk to her with the flight attendant hovering around, catering to his every whim.

After landing, they rode from the private airfield to the hotel and checked in. The glamorous lobby of the George V, with its high ceilings, nineteenth-century paintings, and accent pieces, felt surreal to Vivian, and the feeling intensified when Javier spoke fluently in French to the concierge, who treated him like a VIP.

She frowned when the concierge showed them into the massive and opulent penthouse suite. "I want my own room."

"You have it." Javier pointed to another door. "Separate rooms, same suite."

Vivian walked into her room. The green-and-gold striped walls harmonized with the four-poster bed of rich, dark wood. A private terrace caught her attention, and she opened the French doors to suck in a breath of smoggy Parisian air. She wrinkled her nose. Still, the majestic Eiffel Tower crowned the city skyline with splendor and grace. The sparkling lights on the tower created a ridiculously romantic atmosphere, which made her uncomfortable.

She'd been to Paris once on a high school field trip, but that was years ago, and it had been a very different experience.

Now here she was in the City of Light with a man who undoubtedly hailed from the Dark Ages. A man without a heart.

A man who had killed Molly.

Vivian closed her eyes and remembered why she was here. Her best friend had been there for her through thick and thin. She'd helped Vivian cope with the loss of her parents. Molly's annoying insistence that she get a life outside of school had encouraged Vivian to go on any number of awkward, ill-fated first dates, but at least the dates had given them both something to laugh about afterward. Molly's love for all living things made it a true irony that she had died far before her time.

And Vivian missed her. Every single day.

She startled when a low voice spoke from behind her. "Worried about something?"

Javier stood against the doorframe. While she'd been contemplating the view, he'd changed into a pair of black slacks, a striped shirt, and a dinner jacket. His hair was damp, which meant he'd either showered *very* quickly or she'd been lost in the view for too long.

She shook her head.

"Great. We should get dinner."

"I'm not hungry, Mr. Rivera." She crossed her arms and resumed staring at the view.

Javier closed the gap between them. "Vivian... We are now on a first-name basis, don't you agree?"

"I don't know you well enough." Vivian shot him a glance over her shoulder. "You brought me here against my will. What other option did I have? To be questioned by the police and cross-examined by solicitors? To lose my job over nothing? If you wanted me to come with you, fine. But this is a work assignment for me."

"And who are you working for?" Javier asked.

I'm working for justice. "For you, yet I have no idea how I can be of service in Paris." Unnerved by his proximity, she moved away from him into the room, then realized her mistake. The dimmed lights gave it a note of unwanted intimacy.

"Come with me," Javier said, following her inside.

Vivian sighed.

"We'll talk. And eat. We either go out or do it right here." He stood in the middle of the room. His presence so near the big bed, with its crisp linens and plush pillows, was downright…bothersome.

Just how dangerous was Javier Rivera to her own well-being? She blamed him for Molly's death. It stood to reason she should fear for her own life, too.

But he didn't frighten her. Not in that way.

"I'd rather eat out." Vivian cleared her throat and brushed her neck with her fingers, creating an invisible layer of protection against him.

He can't do any harm in a public place. I hope.

"I knew you'd change your mind." He grinned, and she hated him for having his way.

The swanky restaurant had an upstairs nightclub. Vivian wondered if he'd chosen somewhere more modern and upbeat just so she would look out of place with her saggy ponytail and old suit. All the women within view sported expensive jewelry, sophisticated gowns, and designer handbags.

Some of them smiled at Javier, and Vivian caught one raising her eyebrows at his companion—tall and too-awkward Vivian, with her unflattering clothes and her complete lack of glamour.

"They are jealous of you," Javier said after the waiter left.

Vivian glanced at him across the corner table, feigning a lack of comprehension.

"The women."

"Well, they shouldn't be." She tucked a few loose strands of hair behind her ear.

"That's where you are wrong," Javier said smoothly, his eyes warm and inviting.

"Why, because they think I'm with you?"

"Because you are beautiful."

He made the compliment sound more like an insult, and Vivian didn't know how to take it. His accented words had a primal effect on her, sending a shot of hot liquid through her veins. She'd never known animosity could affect her this way.

Then again, she'd never hated someone as she hated Javier Rivera.

"I have to go to the ladies' room." She rose to her feet, needing to escape him, if only for a moment.

"Of course." He stood immediately.

"I can find my own way."

"I won't let you out of my sight. Deal with it." Javier brushed her elbow with his hand, then dropped behind and shadowed her to the women's restroom door.

"Do you mind?" Vivian rolled her eyes, and although it didn't appear to faze him, he let her enter the restroom without him.

Once she'd escaped Javier, she relaxed, her shoulders dropping from their position by her ears.

She turned the tap to cold and washed her hands before sprinkling some water onto her tired eyes and her neck. Perhaps the cool liquid would soothe her and allay her doubts and fears.

She wouldn't let Javier intimidate her. Not the way he had intimidated Molly.

Vivian turned off the faucet, dried her hands, and patted a paper towel on her face.

Think, Vivian, think. She sighed, looking straight into her reflection in the mirror. Behind her, a janitorial cart held the door of the handicapped stall wide open.

A short woman in a cleaning uniform came out of the stall, mopping the floor.

The woman mumbled a greeting, and Vivian noticed a

mobile phone at the belt of her uniform.

Vivian stepped closer. "I know this will sound strange, but I need your help."

The woman half-smiled, gestured, and replied in French.

"I need to use your mobile." Vivian pointed at the device. "It's an emergency."

The woman shook her head. Vivian grabbed the last pounds she had left in her pocket and handed them to the woman, carefully taking the mobile out of the holder on her belt.

"*S'il vous plaît...*emergency," she pleaded.

The woman counted the money, and Vivian called the phone number she'd memorized.

"It's Vivian," she said when Roger answered, his voice a familiar rasp. "I don't have much time…"

She summarized the past few hours' events.

"You are in Paris with Rivera now? This means the deal will go through sooner than expected. Find a way to search his bedroom for any notes or copies of the contract. I need to know why Broussard has chosen his proposal over mine."

"I'll try."

"Make it happen, Vivian. We need to buy time."

She sighed and leaned her head against the wall, closing her eyes for a moment and massaging her temple with her free hand. "I don't know if I can do this," she murmured, and for a moment, saying it out loud felt better than chocolate. She couldn't ignore her need to share her despair with someone, although she doubted Roger really cared about her feelings. All six months since Molly's funeral, she'd been alone. All those years since her parents' death…

"If you can do what?" Javier's angry voice from behind her made her jump.

Vivian clenched her palm around the mobile at her side, the quickening beating of her heart suffocating any temporary relief she had been feeling. "This is the ladies' room." She turned to him as he stepped closer, the muscle in his jaw jumping, his eyes narrowed. "You shouldn't be here."

"Neither should you." Javier crushed her against the wall, pressing his body against hers. She didn't like the vulnerability that blanketed her or the feel of his muscular thighs against hers, his right hand cupping her own where she clutched the mobile. His unforgiving black eyes hinted he was not someone who walked away from a challenge.

Well, neither am I.

"Get away from me."

"Vivian, open your hand," he demanded.

"No."

Javier glared at her with a frank masculine defiance. With his index finger, he began drawing invisible circles on her hand. She swallowed, cursing the dryness in her throat.

"*Madame et monsieur?*" The cleaning woman coughed.

Javier exchanged a few short sentences with her, his gaze flickering between the mobile nestled in Vivian's hand and the other woman, who spoke abruptly. Although Vivian didn't understand the words, she could tell by the tone that the woman wanted her mobile back and nothing to do with Vivian.

"No, you don't understand," Vivian pleaded.

"Vivian, give her what is rightfully hers. Otherwise we can call the manager, or the police," Javier said. He backed a few steps away from Vivian. "What is it with you and stealing?"

"I was not—" Vivian started, but then sighed. It was no use. With a slight shake of her head, she handed the woman her mobile back.

Javier took a few large bills from his pocket and handed the money to the cleaning woman in exchange for the mobile.

"You bought it from her? Oh, for Pete's sake."

He raised the phone to his ear. "Hello. Who is this?"

His frustrated groan, along with the busy signal a couple of seconds later, gave her momentary relief. He stabbed at the buttons, apparently attempting to call back the number she'd dialed. When he lifted the phone to his ear again, she heard it ringing. Clearly, he'd succeeded in reaching the number, but he was getting no answer. Roger must have heard some of the commotion and decided against picking up.

Javier pocketed the phone. No doubt he'd try to track down the owner of the number later, but she doubted he would succeed. Roger only gave her untraceable prepaid phone numbers.

"Who were you talking to?" Javier asked.

"None of your business."

"This is *exactly* my business," he said under his breath.

"Maybe I have someone I left behind, Mr. Rivera. Weren't you raving about my exquisite beauty a few minutes ago?"

"You are doing this for a man." Javier snorted, a disgusted sound. "And you are involved with him."

"You're twisting my words, Mr. Rivera."

"If you were a man, I'd be twisting your neck." He stepped closer and touched her jaw with the tip of his finger. Her body went completely still, but inside, she seethed with anger. Javier traced his finger down her neck, a hint of satisfaction twisting his curved lips when he found her pulse.

He was so close… His head slightly bowed toward her, and she had to raise her eyes to meet his. The intensity she found there warned her that he could kill her. Or kiss her.

The words played in her head, a perverse symphony. *Kill her. Or kiss her.* Which possibility did she fear more?

Vivian pressed her lips together, looking around for the cleaning woman. Vanished. She glanced at his fingers, which hovered over her neck, almost as if he wanted to touch her but couldn't decide if it was a good idea.

It wasn't.

His fingers trembled. Rage or lust? She couldn't tell. But she wasn't frightened, and that fact scared her more than the look in his eyes.

Vivian swallowed hard and forced herself to move.

"I'm glad I'm not a man, then," she said as she stepped away from him, smoothing her suit jacket to give her shaking fingers something to do.

"Come back to the table," he ordered.

And so she did.

When they'd returned to their seats, Javier asked, "Vivian, why are you doing this? This man is using you to get to me, and I want to know why. What's his name?" He ran his fingers through his cropped hair—a style that exposed his hardened features.

"So you can harass him the same way you've done me? I don't go around asking the names of your lovers, Mr. Rivera."

"My lovers aren't relevant to you." He frowned. "Who's behind this? Rogers? Traveaux?" He hesitated. "Finn?"

"Who are these people?" A man like Javier would have no shortage of enemies in the business world.

Thankfully, the sommelier interrupted and suggested the right wine to accompany dinner. There was even a bread cart, with a different type of bread for each course of their meal.

"Thank you," Javier said to the sommelier.

The waiter brought the appetizer, a delicious caviar cream, and she was able to focus on her meal.

"Did you know Molly Richardson?" Javier asked her after several minutes had passed. "She worked for the Rivera Group."

Vivian sipped her wine to buy a few seconds before answering.

If only she were better at lying… But she had been honest her whole life. She'd even told her parents the truth when they asked if she'd skipped class once to go to the mall with friends.

When a female friend asked if an outfit was too tight or made her butt look bigger, Vivian always told the truth.

She knew that if she admitted she'd known Molly, she put herself in danger. Javier could simply try to make her disappear the same way he'd gotten rid of her friend. Would he?

"Vivian," he said. When her eyes found his again, her stomach clenched. He was so determined. "You know her."

Her fingers tightened around her wineglass. *Hold on to the lie, open up, or a little bit of both?*

She gathered all her strength and anger together. "I know you killed her."

Javier cocked his head in silence for a moment. He frowned. It was the reaction of a man who'd run into someone whose name he couldn't remember.

Then he chuckled. "I killed her?" The mockery in his voice made her want to splash her remaining wine in his face.

"Yes," she continued, pretending to be unaffected.

"Molly Richardson committed suicide."

"It was smart of you to make it seem that way. But I listened to the voice mail you left her." It was paramount for her not to back down. He knew that she knew about Molly. The only leverage she had over him was the scant scrap of evidence she'd managed to gather in the days after Molly's death.

His voice mail.

She could almost hear his angry voice playing over in her mind, again and again, just as fresh as when she had first listened to it. *You'll pay for this, Molly. I'm done with you,* he had said. Knowing Molly's voice mail password had finally served a purpose for Vivian—although the police hadn't cared much. A powerful man like Javier had been smart enough to find an alibi. His money bought everything, didn't it? Well, that was about to change.

The mockery washed from his face, and a hint of sour smile touched his lips. "Is that why you were in my office? If I had killed her, did you think you'd find evidence there?"

"One never knows. People slip up sometimes."

She was counting on Javier to slip. It was a long shot, but one worth taking. After all, the whole evening had escaped her control. Her desire to bring him down was the last secret she could keep.

He narrowed his eyes. "Who did you call?"

"Someone who knows where I am in case something happens to me."

"What is your connection to Molly?" He leaned over the table, his body betraying his interest in her reply.

"We were best friends," she said with pride. "She was like a sister to me."

He nodded. "My condolences. But I didn't have anything to do with it." He straightened his shoulders, and the look on his face told her the subject was closed.

Vivian forced laughter. "You didn't? You slept with her."

He shrugged. "That's hardly a crime."

"No. I suppose sleeping with you was just a bad judgment call on her part." Vivian cleared her throat. "What about having her watched and followed?"

"I paid a private investigator to find out who she was selling information to," he said coolly. "In case you don't know, your beloved friend was involved in industrial espionage. She tried to steal insider information and was probably planning to sell it to the highest bidder."

Investigated. Stalked. Threatened. It's just a matter of semantics for him, isn't it? A man like Javier Rivera doesn't simply confess to a crime.

"Is that why you hired those two men to follow her everywhere? Is that why one of them physically threatened her?"

"What men? I didn't hire anyone to scare her," he said firmly.

"Are you telling me your private investigator acted on his own without your knowledge because you didn't care to know the details?"

His eyes were hard now, flashing with annoyance. Perhaps he'd started to realize that backing down wasn't an option for her. She didn't know if that was good or bad, safe or dangerous.

Their orders arrived—lobster in the shell with avocado sauce for her and a tender fillet braised in red sauce for him. She couldn't eat with the tight knot forming in her stomach. She had to keep going.

The waiter left, and Vivian pressed Javier. "The day she died, she called me. We were supposed to meet the next day. You said on your voice mail that she would pay."

He let out a long, deep sigh. His eyes left hers for a moment as he thought about his answer. Or plotted a way to change her mind. "I meant professionally. She was done working for me or any other reputable company if I had any say in it. And I had every right to be mad at her."

Vivian shook her head, unsatisfied with his answer. "I'm determined, Mr. Rivera. You won't get rid of me easily."

"I don't want to." Javier traced long fingers on the rim of the wineglass. "Keep your friends close and your enemies closer, isn't that how it goes?" His voice had turned husky, his eyes sweeping over her face.

"What do you mean?"

He cut into the meat. "After what you just told me, I won't let you go around telling these lies about me. I could sue you for defamation, but I'd rather keep you close until I can convince you that you're wrong about me."

"An enticing prospect, but I can't give you my entire life."

"The weekend. If you aren't convinced I didn't kill Molly by Monday, I will let you go."

No doubt Monday was the day he would sign his merger deal. It made sense. They were in Paris. He wanted to avoid any scandal until his merger went through.

She'd considered making a scandal of her own, once. But after much consideration, Vivian had changed her mind. Going to the media against a big shot like Javier wouldn't do her any good. She had tried the police, but they couldn't help her because Javier had an alibi for the time when Molly had supposedly killed herself. If Vivian had tried to get the media's attention, Javier would have used the resources at his disposal to make her look bad.

She knew he would do it, too. In a heartbeat.

"What if I don't want to stay?"

"I will give my solicitor and the police that call I should have made a few hours ago."

"And if I'm not convinced by the end of the weekend?"

He smiled. "That won't be the case." Javier drew his eyes from hers as he pulled out his mobile and read from the screen. "Vivian May Foster. Twenty-six years old, no siblings, has a college degree in arts. Born in upstate New York, moved to England at age seven."

She raised the fork to her mouth and began to eat. How long would it take him to link her to Roger? Javier had power, resources, and an investigator who was obviously already on her tail.

"Why did you apply for a receptionist job? Couldn't you put your degree to better use?" Before she could answer, he added, "You didn't need this job."

Her heart raced. *Careful, Vivian.* She had to watch every word. His offer to spend the weekend with her had restored her hope of using his nearness to her advantage. If she succeeded in getting information to Roger, he would act quickly, and Javier would lose the billion-pound merger he'd worked hard for. Money was all that mattered to a man like

Javier, which meant it was all they could take away from him. He had to lose, one way or another.

"I took the job to see if I could find out more about you." Telling him that much didn't compromise her.

"Amuse me, Vivian. What have you learned?"

"You're usually at work by eight. You entertain business associates at the new steakhouse a couple of blocks from the office. You also travel internationally every couple days or so, which drives your live-in concierge nuts because she never knows if you'll be able to make it for dinner."

"You've talked to Mrs. Hough?" He chuckled.

"I only transferred calls. But I gathered as much."

He kept looking at her, assessing her from top to bottom. "You are quite the stalker, Vivian."

She shifted in her seat. "Don't flatter yourself."

"Who was the person you called?"

"Are you planning on causing me some harm, Mr. Rivera? Is that why you want to know the identity of the person who can testify against you?" She was pleased with how confident she sounded.

"Looking at you, Vivian, I can think of a couple of things I could do to you, but they aren't illegal by Parisian standards." Javier's gaze slid from her face to her neck and then to her breasts. "Or British standards."

She inhaled sharply, forcing herself to ignore his teasing. He wanted to make her feel awkward, didn't he? Vulnerable. Out of place.

"This lobster is magnificent," she said.

They finished their meal in silence, and she managed to avoid looking at Javier all the way from the restaurant to their room. In the limousine on the drive back to the hotel, she sat as far away from him as possible.

But the dead silence had its own weight, and Vivian decided she preferred his Spanish-Inquisition-like questions.

He followed her every move with his eyes as he walked through the hotel alongside her. Vivian usually didn't walk quickly, but she wanted to get back to her elegant prison. She wanted to get away from Javier.

"We'll continue our conversation tomorrow," he said as they reached her bedroom.

Vivian nodded and locked the door behind her.

She took a shower, the powerful jets spraying her with steamy water. Vivian washed the soap off her skin for several minutes and wished the shower would give her body a clean slate. She wanted nothing more than to forget Javier's unwanted touch, the heat of his stare.

She would never have believed it if someone had told her she'd end her day in a luxury hotel in Paris, being closely watched by none other than Javier Rivera.

But now she had to get used to it…and start thinking about how she would take advantage of the situation. At least she'd been able to tell Roger where she was.

Roger. It wasn't his name, of course. She knew almost nothing about him, and she preferred it that way.

She'd met Roger only once, after Molly's death, when he'd approached her and asked her to take Molly's place and assist him in taking the merger away from Javier.

Vivian didn't know what Javier had done to Roger. Certainly, the older Scottish gentleman was no saint himself. He wanted information about the merger—wanted to take Javier Rivera out of the running—and he had no scruples about using two women who craved revenge to get what he wanted.

As long as Roger helped her, Vivian didn't care.

With his help, she'd been hired at the Rivera office. She had studied the security system, the positioning of the cameras, and Javier's routine. And when the rumor about the merger became water-cooler gossip, both Vivian and

Roger had agreed it was time to start looking for concrete information. Contracts, notes, dates. Anything would help.

Vivian stepped out of the shower and grabbed a fluffy, monogrammed hotel robe.

By the time her hair was dry, the rest of the suite had fallen silent.

She opened her door far enough to check the hallway and living room lights. They were all off.

Vivian tiptoed out of her room. The open drapes framed the seductive full moon outside, its light shining into the otherwise dark common area of the suite.

Perhaps Javier is a heavy sleeper. She didn't waste time imagining his frankly male body sprawled on a large bed. Sleeping or awake, it didn't matter to her. She needed to get in touch with Roger again.

Making calls from her room wasn't an option, because the number would show on the bill. She would have to use a guest phone in the lobby. Roger would know exactly what to do and how to move her plan forward.

The door at the end of the hall was closed. She stretched out her hand to open it.

Suddenly, a cold metal bracelet clutched her wrist, and she heard a clicking noise.

Vivian screamed. She turned to face her assailant, a dreadful chill racing up her spine.

"Going somewhere?" Javier stood bare-chested by her side. She raised her eyes to his.

"You frightened me." Vivian let her breath out slowly. When she moved her hand to touch her chest, her wrist caught.

She looked down. She was handcuffed to Javier.

"What are you doing?" She shook her hand, bouncing the short chain between their wrists. "Take these off," she shouted, shaking her hand again.

This can't be happening...

"I've known you for a few hours, and this is the third time I've seen you do something you don't care to explain," Javier said, his eyes accusing her.

"I wanted to get some fresh air. What kind of man would ambush a virtual stranger in the middle of the night to handcuff her?"

What else does he have planned?

"Consider it a security measure to make sure you don't go anywhere," Javier said casually. "Tomorrow there will be a bodyguard here to watch you while I take care of an important matter."

"I don't need a bodyguard."

"He will make sure you are looked after."

"Yes, my well-being is high on your priority list, isn't it?" Vivian pulled the chain.

"Of course, *mi querida.*" Javier flashed a crooked grin.

"Then take this off. It's making my skin itch."

"You'll get used to it," Javier said, moving toward her bedroom.

Vivian balked. She didn't want to get used to the handcuffs, or to share a bed with Javier. "Is that an expert's advice?" She wished she could wipe the cynical smile right off his face. "Actually, I don't want to know."

"Come to bed, Vivian," he demanded.

"No." She raised her voice.

"There's no option. A quick call, and my lawyers will be on you. Even the cleaning lady can be a witness to your reckless behavior." His voice was emotionless.

Vivian stopped short, recognizing the truth of what he said. Determined to see Javier get what he deserved, she refused to let the chance to teach him a lesson slip through her fingers. If spending a night by his side was part of the package, she would deal with it. Somehow.

"Can't you at least wear a shirt?" She stumbled along beside him into her bedroom.

She'd avoided looking at him before. Now, with the bedside lamp on, it was hard to ignore the well-muscled arms, the strong, broad shoulders framing his chiseled chest. Her gaze slid downward, catching a tantalizing glimpse of dark hair disappearing into dark blue, silky pajama pants.

"You should be glad I had these on. I usually sleep in the nude," he said nonchalantly.

Vivian knotted her robe as tightly as she could. "This is outrageous."

Javier gently pulled her to the bed and turned down the covers. Goose bumps rose on her arms as awareness of what was about to happen sunk in. It had been a while since she'd been intimate with a man. Her last lover had been an art merchant she dated for a while. But that had been a relationship…and this was pure torture. This large, commanding Spaniard made the worst jerk she'd ever dated seem as sweet as a basket of puppies by comparison.

"We're just sleeping." Her voice trembled against her will. "No funny business."

"You have my word." Javier flashed a smile and signaled for her to get in bed first. "I'll behave."

"You'd better." Vivian leaned onto the bed, her mind racing as he followed suit.

His laughter was rich and sarcastic. "Vivian, if I had a hidden agenda, I could think of a few women who wouldn't mind obliging."

"I pity them." She sighed. "Poor women, wasting their time with a man who's not fulfilling their needs."

He sat next to her, stretched out his legs, and lay down on the bed. Vivian moved close to the edge to ensure a safe distance, hoping her limbs wouldn't rub against his. Sharing a bed with him was so disturbing and intimate.

"I can guarantee you, Vivian, I know a thing or two about fulfilling a woman's needs." His diabolical grin did nothing to dampen her inner turmoil.

"I was talking about having a committed relationship, Mr. Rivera." She pulled a pillow close to her and punched it several times with her free hand, wishing she could do the same to the man by her side. *All in good time…*

"I take it you are the committing kind?"

"My love life is off-limits for discussion. Sharing a bed with you is bad enough." She punched her pillow one last time.

"We'll see about that." He turned the lamp off, their hands lightly rubbing as he moved. "Good night, Vivian."

"Tomorrow, I'll wake up and realize this was all a terrible nightmare," she said, and the last thing she heard before drifting off to sleep was his low laughter.

Javier observed the strand of light shining through the drapes from the full moon. Aside from it, the room was dark. The intrusive beam of light outlined the dangerous curves of Vivian's sleeping body.

Was it just his imagination? Was the light powerful enough to shine from her wavy hair down to her dark red manicured toes?

Javier clenched his jaw.

When he had ordered the concierge to deliver a pair of handcuffs to his room in a rush, he'd been certain the efficient employee had imagined they'd be put to an entirely different use than what Javier in mind. He was glad luxury hotel concierges were reliable when it came to unusual VIP requests.

Vivian could not be allowed to escape.

Though her accusation that he had killed Molly had surprised him at first, his shock had quickly given way to caution. Vivian could become a huge liability for his merger, as the media loved this kind of sensationalism. He couldn't let her frolic on the streets of Paris—or London, for that matter—until he'd secured the deal with Broussard.

He remembered the hot intensity in her eyes when she'd accused him, but he doubted the truth of what she'd told him. No one would put herself on the line for the memory of her best friend—no one would jeopardize her own security, invest the time, face charges if he took it that far.

He did know, though, that Vivian Foster was strong, and she wasn't collapsing. The intensity of her strength challenged him, aroused him, and bothered him.

Did she want money? He'd offered her money. Did she want more?

His thoughts were interrupted by a jerk on his cuffed wrist.

"No…" she said, shaking her head from side to side.

"Vivian." She didn't react to his voice.

She was probably still sleeping. Her breath caught. Javier was about to close his eyes when she moved again.

"No," she repeated.

He tapped her shoulder to wake her up, but all she did was sway against him, shaking her head from side to side.

Javier tensed, wondering whether to turn on the light and wake her up. He eased his weight onto the mattress with his elbows, then turned to his side and faced her shadow. What did he know about the decorum of waking up a woman from her nightmare? Especially a woman who was his prisoner.

"It's okay." He caressed her cheek with the back of his hand, her soft skin making his own skin tingle in response. He'd experienced many nightmares as a child, but he'd seldom received the comfort he craved. He had feared walking into his mother's room and waking his stepfather—the source of his nightmares.

As her mumbling continued, he brushed a few stray strands of her hair from her face. A stab of tenderness made his heart ache, and he had to fight the impulse to run his long fingers through her auburn tresses and hold her tight.

"No…" He heard her broken voice, and although she was still asleep, he took it as advice.

No. She was not his lover.

"Shh," he whispered, and her mumbling began to fade.

As soon as her shoulders relaxed, he pulled his hand away and moved to the far side of the bed.

She was not his lover.

The Broussard merger would ensure that he got to the place he'd wanted to be for a long time. He'd learned at a very early age that a man's success was measured by his achievements, by his financial profits. The long years he'd endured child abuse, hatred, and neglect within his own family were behind him. He'd made himself into a new person, alienating those who had doubted he could ever succeed on his own. Many dreamed of acquiring the empire Broussard had spent his lifetime amassing, but Javier would be the one to take it, just as he'd taken whatever he wanted since that rainy autumn afternoon when he'd left his home in Spain forever.

No one would stand in his way. He would ignore the thoughts that crept into his mind when he least expected them. Thoughts of her endless long legs wrapped around his torso, her head tossing back as she moaned with him thrusting deep into her…

Enough!

Vivian Foster was cloaked in a veil of mystery, and he couldn't wait to strip her naked.

Chapter Three

"Rise and shine."

Vivian heard the powerful voice from far away. Mumbling in reply, she buried her face deeper into the pillow and hugged it tight with both arms. "Wake up, Vivian."

With a sigh, she rolled across the bed. Reaching the other side, she half-opened her eyes with a yawn, her cheek lingering against the silkiness of the goose-feather pillows. She was so relaxed and...free, she realized as she stretched her arm.

The handcuffs were gone. Vivian opened her eyes with a start.

She touched her wrist with the other hand, her fingers wrapping around her skin to make sure this was not a dream. A chuckle from disturbingly close by startled her, and Vivian glanced over her shoulder to see Javier, fully clothed in an elegant, dark-blue business suit, sitting on the edge of the bed with a wicked look on his face.

She sat up at once, blushing when she noticed her robe had come loose in the night and exposed the valley of fair skin between her breasts. "What's happening?" She crossed her arms.

"I have business to take care of, and you could use some pampering." Javier's drawl was smooth as silk.

Her eyes lit on a beautifully set breakfast tray, complete with a range of cheeses, breads and jam, rich pastries, juices, and coffee. "Oh, room service!"

He looked toward the door, and three smiling women entered her room, all wearing the monogrammed uniform of hotel employees. "You will have a spa day. I also asked to have some clothes brought up for you."

She wouldn't argue about clothes. She needed them. Well, perhaps not this kind of clothes, Vivian realized as the women brought several cases into her room. There were makeup containers, a folded massage table, and a swiveling rack full of glamorous dresses. Shoeboxes with designer labels were stacked at the bottom of the rack.

She blinked when she spotted sexy nightgowns hanging on the rack and recognized a luxurious lingerie store logo on one of the closed boxes. "That's a bit much."

"You'll need something to wear for a couple more days." He stood up. "I'll be unavailable the whole day." His next comment poured cold water on her lovely distraction. "There's a bodyguard outside."

"I'm trapped in here." Vivian made a face and looked down at her hands. Though the handcuffs were gone, she was as much a prisoner as she'd been the previous night, with no access to his room or any of the other rooms. How could she hunt for clues about the merger if she was stuck in here?

His smile didn't reach his eyes. "Vivian, this is hardly a trap. You will be pampered, and in the evening I will stop by and take you to dinner and finish that conversation we started."

"I can hardly wait." Vivian watched as a woman unfolded the massage table and began to set the mood by dimming the lights and opening a bottle of oil. The scent of lavender filled the room.

"I like you better when you're sleeping." He headed to the door.

Vivian snorted. *Whatever that meant…*

She had to think of a way to get into his room. But with a bodyguard at her door and the aestheticians hovering around, what could she do? She pondered the problem as they analyzed her skin to decide what kind of facial she'd have. Vivian had not had so many people working on her since… well, ever.

They gave her a pedicure, buffed her nails, and waxed her eyebrows with military precision. The hairstylist offered options for a new haircut, but Vivian settled for a trim and blow dry. She already had too many changes in her life. She didn't need to radically alter her look, too.

The stylist asked her to try on some of the party dresses and casual outfits to ensure that the sizing was right. Vivian sighed and went along. She raised an eyebrow when the stylist brought out a long, one-shouldered red gown.

The gown was beautiful, and it made her feel like royalty, with layers of silk falling asymmetrically down her body from an empire waistline. It hinted at her curves without making them too obvious. Vivian couldn't help but smile. She had never worn anything so decadent and beautiful.

"Is that the dress you will wear for the fund-raising party, mademoiselle?" the stylist asked.

"The fund-raising party?"

What party? Javier had said he would drop by to continue their chat in the evening and take her to dinner. He'd said nothing about a party.

Of course, Vivian realized. He would probably be in meetings related to the big merger all day. He had used the spa day and the new clothes to distract her… She figured he'd told the stylist to bring her clothes, and the woman had assumed she was one of his many lovers. The truth was, he didn't intend to take her with him to the party. He would go by himself, or with another woman, and probably later he would drop by to escort her to dinner as he had told her he would—just when she was about to burst with cabin fever.

"It's tonight?" Vivian asked.

"Yes, mademoiselle. Everyone is getting ready." The stylist grabbed a couple of high heels from different boxes and showed them to Vivian, holding them close to the dress.

"Because the party will be at the hotel?"

The older beautician shot the stylist a subtle warning look and spoke a curt sentence in French.

"Who is the ball for, again? I'm sure Javier mentioned, but it must have slipped my mind." Vivian put her hand to her forehead, as if making an effort to remember.

"I'm not sure." The stylist looked away.

Was she paranoid, or had Javier told the beauty team not to talk to her about anything other than facials and color coordinating?

Vivian smiled. "Not to worry. I'll find out soon."

Other body and facial treatments filled the rest of her long spa day. The novelty of caviar-based facials and hot stone massages wore off quickly. The massage should have soothed her nerves, but instead it only unsettled her. If the comments made by the masseuse were anything to go by, the knot in her stomach must have worked its way up to her shoulders and neck. But how could she relax when she had made no progress? She couldn't let any opportunity slide between her now-hydrated, French-tipped manicured fingers.

The last of the spa employees left right after a small fruity snack had been brought up to the room. The sky outside had begun to shift, the afternoon sunlight fading as the dinner hour arrived. The room became blissfully quiet.

An hour later, Vivian looked at her reflection in the full-length mirror. The red dress complemented her skin, her hair fell loose over her shoulders in lustrous waves, and although her makeup had seemed a bit much when they applied it, now she appreciated the effect. The dark, smoky eye shadow made her eye color stand out, her lips appeared red-hot and sultry, and her cheeks had a soft pink flush.

She walked to the entrance of her room and saw a large man in a dark suit sitting on a chair in front of her bedroom door.

"Let's go." Vivian headed toward the exit, setting an impatient pace. The bodyguard quickly placed himself between her and the door. "Mr. Rivera gave me express orders not to let you out of my sight."

"Good, because I'm on my way to see him." She tossed her hair behind her shoulder.

The man scratched his short beard. "He told me he'd come pick you up. He said nothing about you going anywhere."

Vivian laughed. "I wouldn't be surprised. Men! They just can't handle the details sometimes."

The guard stared at her in silence.

"I was getting ready the whole day for the fund-raising ball downstairs, and you have to accompany me to it. You can take me to your boss yourself."

"I don't think—"

"Unless of course you want me to tell him that you made me late. He hates tardiness." Vivian rested both hands on her hips. "What's it going to be?"

Vivian crossed the entrance of the salon with the bodyguard, adrenaline pumping through her veins. She'd pulled it off. She had no idea what to do next, but one of the things she'd decided in the past twenty-four hours was that improvising was a skill she would master by the time she returned to England.

Would she gain access to privileged information by the end of the night? Would she catch a break and find an opportunity to return undetected to Javier's room for a quick search? She didn't know. The possibilities were endless. But she was sure her odds were better if she wasn't stuck inside her room, powerless as a china doll.

They reached the narrow area where a well-coiffed blonde asked their names to check against the guest list. The bodyguard said something in French that made her nod and leave immediately.

In a couple of minutes, the woman reappeared with Javier, who wore crisp black tie. The perfection of the suit's lines highlighted his manly frame. Although his hair was sleek and his face freshly shaved, he appeared far from calm. No, the glint of surprise in his eyes when he saw her quickly shifted into a blazing fury.

"Vivian. What are you doing here?" He stepped close, speaking under his breath.

"I was all dressed up with nowhere to go." She smiled, ignoring the trembling in her hands.

Javier and the bodyguard exchanged a few sentences in French. She could see by Javier's expression he was blaming the bodyguard for letting her out of the suite and nearly into the party.

Javier turned to her again. "You shouldn't be here."

"Well, why should I be locked up in that room while you live the high life?" Her gaze wandered past him to the sea of well-dressed guests dancing and strolling across an elegant ballroom.

"I told you I would take you out later. Now go back to your room." He tried to lead her away.

"Mr. Rivera, I will cause a scandal right here if you make me go. I will scream at the top of my lungs. How will that look for you?" Vivian glanced around at the elegantly clad guests walking through the main ballroom door.

He pulled back, his eyes sending her a message that carried a threat and a promise. This man wasn't used to being told what to do, and he didn't like it much.

"You want to live the high life?" He shot her a sexy smile and closed the gap between them, leaning close. "Okay. But you will not leave my side."

"Deal."

They walked into the ballroom alone. Apparently Javier didn't want to draw attention to himself. The bodyguard retreated to a safe location just inside the tall wooden doors, where he could watch from a distance.

The ballroom was enormous, lavishly decorated with white lilies and scented vanilla candles. Low lighting created an intimate feel. The hundred or so guests were sophisticated, the women mostly older than Vivian and quite refined, with expensive-looking jewelry, silky gowns, and haute couture clutches that probably cost a small fortune.

The men were also older, impeccably dressed in black tie. She hated to admit it, but Javier was more charismatic and powerful than anyone else in the ballroom, and completely in his element. He belonged there more than she had ever belonged anywhere.

Well, I belong here. At least for now.

"What kind of charity fund-raiser is this?" Vivian glanced at the tables, all set with more silverware than she knew what to do with.

"It benefits women who have been abused," he said. She spun around to look at him. He wore a poker face—expressionless—and she wondered how he could talk so casually about a subject that should haunt his conscience after what he'd done to Molly.

"Really?" she asked. "Emotional abuse as well?"

"I suppose." Javier frowned.

How ironic.

As he guided her to their table, his hand firm on her bare back, Vivian attempted to focus on anything other than the brush of his fingers on her skin. She glanced at the five-tier chandelier that hung over a larger table at the front of the room, the long purple vases that contrasted with the white lilies and candles. She inhaled, wanting to relish the smoky vanilla scent, but Javier's minty aftershave overpowered her senses, and his fingers left a trail of tingles where they pressed into her bare flesh.

Vivian stiffened when his hand moved gently up her shoulder blade, circling around the small tattoo she'd had inscribed on her back after her parents' death.

"What does this mean?" he whispered from behind her, closing the gap between them.

Her pulse quickened. "It means *family* in Japanese."

"I wouldn't take you for the family type." He moved around to face her, holding her wrist as if waiting for an answer.

"I could say the same about you," she managed to say.

"Why don't you have any emergency contacts in your employee file?"

"I don't need to trouble anyone in the event of an emergency," Vivian said truthfully. She didn't have anyone to call. Not anymore.

"Not even your parents?" Javier pressed, loosening his grip on her wrist.

"My parents died in a car crash when I was seventeen."

"Did they leave anyone behind besides you?"

"I lost everyone who mattered."

"My condolences," he murmured, his hand rubbing lightly

over her back.

Vivian looked deep into his eyes. The usual arrogance that crowned his hardened features was gone. With a sigh, she resumed walking, and soon they reached their table at the front, close to the raised podium. She smiled as a few guests greeted Javier, wishing she knew who these people were, if they were business partners, acquaintances, or friends. Javier Rivera wasn't known for having many friends.

An older gentleman with a trimmed beard approached the group, and everyone at the table greeted him warmly.

"And who is your charming companion, Javier?" The old man smiled at her.

"This is Vivian Foster. Vivian, meet…" Javier hesitated.

"Call me Edouard." The man kissed her on both cheeks in the French style. *"Enchanté."*

"Nice to meet you, too," Vivian replied. The man exuded wisdom and sympathy.

Javier snaked his hand around her waist, possessively bringing her closer. Her throat closed in discomfort. All she could think about was escaping from his embrace.

"Where have you been hiding this lovely lady?" Edouard asked Javier.

"Oh, we're not…" Vivian shook her head as a red wave of anger spread over her face.

"You'd be surprised to know where *she* was hiding." If there was humor in Javier's voice, his fingers tightening around her waist told a different story.

The band played vintage Nina Simone, and elegantly dressed people crowded the dance floor.

"Would you give me the pleasure of this dance, mademoiselle?" Edouard asked her.

"Unfortunately, I was just about to ask her the same," Javier said. His tone was playful, but Vivian had no doubt of the message. He'd meant it when he'd said she was not to leave his side.

But being by his side was dangerous. Literally. The side of her chest crushed against him, his fingertips bit into her dress, and his hot breath was so close. Her awareness of him was a liability she couldn't afford. "I would love to dance, Edouard." Vivian withdrew from Javier's arm.

"But *mi querida*," Javier insisted, his dark eyes sending her a warning message, intense and secretive. Obviously, he didn't want her to go, which only made her more eager to dance with Edouard. Might he know Monsieur Broussard or have information about Javier's agenda in Paris?

"Don't worry," Edouard said. "Just one dance, and I will bring her back to you safe and sound." He chuckled, seemingly oblivious to the tension emanating from them both.

"Well, since it's just one dance," Javier said with a tight smile.

As the Frenchman led her to the dance floor, she shot Javier a mocking glance over her shoulder.

"I hope Javier doesn't mind my whisking you away," Edouard said. He raised his hands to meet hers and began dancing elegantly. Vivian did her best to follow him, imagining how odd the two of them had to look together. She was a foot taller than her dance partner.

"I doubt it." She smiled, making a clumsy effort not to trip over his feet. "Have you known him long?"

"I've bumped into him quite a few times. I guess that's the curse of the business world."

"You're doing business with him?" A ripple of excitement traveled through her. *Finally, I'm getting somewhere.*

"Why, my dear?" Edouard swirled her around. "Should I expect you to oversell his potential?"

Vivian chuckled. "I wouldn't be the right person for that."

"Why not?" He spun her around the floor. "You find it impossible to separate matters of the heart from business decisions?"

"It's rather complicated." *The underestimation of the century.*

"Oh, *ma chérie*, it's always complicated."

Edouard sobered, and a moment later he added, "At the risk of sounding odd, I must tell you something."

"Go ahead." Vivian held her breath. There was something about this man that assured her she could trust him.

"You remind me of my daughter." His eyes were filled with pain.

"Do I?" Vivian exhaled slowly. "Is she here today?"

"She's right there." He pointed to the life-size picture above the stage of a beautiful young woman wearing white, her smile broad and her eyes blue. The golden frame was thick, and as Vivian's gaze drifted over the picture, she saw the birth and death dates.

Dead. His daughter was dead.

"I'm sorry." The idea of asking him for any information about Javier vanished from her mind. She would offer him the only thing she could—her silent sympathy for the remainder of the dance.

But Edouard spoke again. "Why is it complicated?"

After a moment's hesitation, she whispered, "Do you know anything about the Broussard merger?"

He hesitated, and his brows furrowed. "I've heard rumors."

Vivian chewed on her lower lip, undecided. Edouard had confided in her, hadn't he? Why couldn't she do the same? She couldn't afford to waste time.

"I need to talk to Monsieur Broussard. I must tell him he can't do business with Javier."

She felt the old man's grip on her tighten. "Why not?"

"I believe he's responsible for my friend's death. Her name was Molly Richardson. I don't think Monsieur Broussard will want to mix up the empire it took him a lifetime to build with someone like Javier."

"That's a very strong accusation."

"I have strong reasons to believe it," she said, thinking of what Molly had told her, and of the voice mail. "I'll tell him everything I know. Do you know how I can get in touch with him?"

Before Edouard could answer, Javier approached them, shooting Edouard a friendly smile. The song had ended. "Can I steal her back?" As the old man nodded, Javier bowed to her, his smile fading and his black eyes drilling into hers.

"Vivian, it's been a pleasure." Edouard bowed to her, handing her to Javier. "And don't worry about stepping on my feet. I will take care of it." Edouard winked. Javier seemed not to notice the hidden message in his last sentence.

Edouard would help her somehow. She could feel it.

"I'm done dancing," she said after Edouard had left. She tried to move away, but Javier wouldn't have it.

"I insist." He splayed his large hand firmly on her bare back, pulling her against him with such strength, she pressed her lips closed to suppress a gasp. "I lead with my right foot, and you follow with your left." He led with a blend of refinement and virility, leaving no doubt this would be a very different dance from the one she had shared with Edouard.

"Opposite sides," she replied sharply. It helped to remind herself out loud where they both stood, just in case the heat coiling low in her stomach tried to trick her. "Got it."

The slow rhythm of the music made it impossible for her to create a buffer zone. Her body molded to his without her consent, her blood thickening and her nipples hardening against the silky fabric of her dress.

Vivian couldn't speak. She tilted her head to the side, battling her yearning to rest it on Javier's shoulder and relax, just for one moment…

If only she could. If only he were anyone else.

He broke the silence. "The deal was, you were to be by my side at all times."

Vivian she stepped back to meet the darkness of his eyes. "It was only a dance." She stopped moving, but he placed his hands on her lower back, gently tapping his fingers.

"Just a dance?" he murmured sarcastically. "With one of the most powerful men in France?"

"How would I know? Maybe in your world he's some kind of hotshot. To me, he was just Edouard, a kind old man who asked me to dance."

"So what did you and the kind old man talk about?"

"Pleasantries. It's nice to talk to someone rational for a change."

"You don't waste time, do you, Vivian? Befriending an old billionaire widower, vulnerable to a beautiful young woman's affection."

"Watch your tone, Mr. Rivera. If you don't begin respecting women, one day you'll be the old lonely man yourself."

"Oh, but I do respect women," Javier said casually, sending her into a twirl so swift that before she could think, she was back in his arms. A couple dancing next to them cheered with excitement at his perfect timing.

"In every way?" she asked coolly. "Have you ever bedded a married woman, for instance?"

"No," he said immediately, tightening his hand on hers.

"Do you think it's appropriate to sleep with an employee?" Vivian locked her gaze on his, challenging him to reveal the real man behind the facade.

"Is this a question or an invitation?" His eyes trailed down her face, assessing her with the intimacy of a caress.

No. No. He'd gotten it all wrong… She wasn't challenging him to bed her.

"A question, obviously."

"It really sounded like an invitation." His lips turned up in a tempting smile as he tightened his hold on her.

"It should have sounded like an accusation. You slept with Molly." She would not forget what had brought her here. Would not forgive.

He sobered. "She was the only employee I ever slept with."

"Were the other employees wiser?"

To her surprise, he threw his head back and laughed. "Vivian, you amuse me."

"That's me, a natural-born entertainer."

"You are not attracted to me?" Javier's condescending smile proved his ego couldn't be dented.

The nerve of the man. He obviously thought no one was immune to his charms.

She shook her head vehemently. "No."

"Then we have nothing to worry about."

She lifted her chin. "Absolutely nothing."

Javier's drawl thickened as he said, "And that makes it all the more interesting."

"Where were you on the evening of her death?"

"Her suicide," he corrected. "I was at a friend's cocktail party."

There was something about the way he danced elegantly while responding to questions about a murder… He remained at ease, but his face displayed a measure of annoyance.

"Which wasn't very far from Molly's flat. You could have gone and returned," Vivian said.

"How do you know where the party was?"

Vivian sighed. She couldn't tell him Roger had helped her to get that information. "I'm resourceful."

He stopped moving for a moment. "What if I give you the names of the people I talked to at the party?"

"You would do that?"

"As long as you call them and pretend to be some jealous girlfriend making sure I behaved. I can't have you telling people I'm a suspect in that crazy mind of yours."

Vivian pondered. There was always the possibility he would give her a list of people who would corroborate his version whether it was true or not. But for the first time, her mind seriously considered the alternative. What if he hadn't done it? What if one of his men had, and he really hadn't given permission or even known? Did he know now? Was he protecting the real murderer?

Either way, it was too soon to tell. She needed more information.

"I'm not crazy," she said, staring deep into his eyes.

To her relief, he said nothing. As the song ended, they returned to their table, and the waitstaff served dinner. Vivian picked at the ice-poached oysters and salmon with wild rice she'd been served. Her stomach was unsettled, and it had nothing to do with the food, which was exquisite. It had everything to do with the man sitting next to her.

Sharing the table with a few other people should have helped. She'd hoped they would mention something business-related, but to her frustration, they all spoke French or Italian. No one, including Javier, made an effort to speak to her. It was as if they saw her as his flavor of the month. Why would they want to get to know her better? She wasn't famous, rich, or strikingly beautiful. And given their situation, she could understand why he didn't want her to mingle with anyone at the table, which was possibly why he hadn't paid her any attention over the course of the meal.

The waiter brought dessert, a small, warm chocolate cake surrounded by wild berries. Vivian ate it with satisfaction, enjoying the sensation of the smooth, warm chocolate filling moving down her throat and the sugar hit that took her thoughts from Javier, even if only for a few moments. When she had finished the dessert, he looked at her with amusement.

"It's my weakness," Vivian said, licking her lips. "Besides, dessert is the best part."

Her light comment didn't have the intended result. The amusement washed out of his face. He observed her with curved lips, and electricity surged through her body when her eyes met his heated stare.

"Have mine," he offered, and as Vivian opened her mouth to decline, Javier scooped a piece up with his fork and dipped it inside her mouth.

Vivian swallowed the morsel and grabbed for her water glass. "Thank you, but I can feed myself." She drank quickly.

"I don't mind," he insisted, and once again he raised his fork to her mouth.

Vivian looked back into his eyes, aware she needed a witty comeback to dispel the sexual tension. She knew he was challenging her. Hadn't he asked her, not long ago, if she was attracted to him? She'd said no. Because that was the truth, wasn't it? So why would she act like a Victorian virgin just because he wanted to give her another piece of paradise?

And by paradise, she only meant chocolate cake.

Delicious, inviting, warm…cake.

Vivian opened her mouth wide. He placed the cake inside once more and smiled.

With his thumb, he took a crumb from the corner of her mouth and brought it to his lips. Vivian caught her breath. Truth be told, she had never seen sexier, fuller lips on a man before. Plump and sensuous, they were just right.

The tip of his tongue slipped out, and he licked the crumb off his finger. She watched him, unable to take her eyes from his mouth.

"You are right. Dessert is the best part." His voice was husky, filled with wickedness.

Vivian blinked a couple of times. What was happening to

her? For the second time this evening, she'd completely lost her head around Javier. No thinking, just feeling. She wasn't used to that kind of indulgence.

Just because she'd lied to Javier about what she was doing in the office when he found her didn't mean she had mastered fooling herself. A part of her was attracted to him.

No good will come of this.

Vivian tore her eyes away, frustrated with herself. Apart from wanting—needing—to take the merger away from him, she now had to remain alert in order to keep her own responsive body in check.

A few short speeches were made, and the audience alternated between attentive listening and clapping for the next speaker. Her fingers played with a long allium stem from the table arrangement.

Edouard walked to the podium amid a standing ovation. Following Javier's lead, she got to her feet and clapped. The lights dimmed, and a large monitor began playing a video about the foundation. The narrator spoke French, but English subtitles appeared on the screen. Sighing in relief, Vivian read them and learned about the man who had founded the charity for women who were victims of domestic violence and abuse.

She gasped when his name flashed on the screen. The founder was called Jean Edouard Broussard.

Monsieur Broussard.

A frozen liquid spread through her bloodstream. She had danced, laughed, and shared a painful moment with the famous Monsieur Broussard—a spirited, kind man who had founded a charity to honor his deceased daughter. She cleared her throat, conscious that Javier was looking at her. "You could have told me he was the host of the fund-raiser."

"Suddenly he's not just a kind old man?" Javier squinted. "What difference does it make to know he's the legendary Jean Edouard Broussard?" he asked in an accusing tone.

"I still don't know him from Adam. But now that I know he's the host, I'm embarrassed. I stepped on his feet so many times."

"I'm sure he's insured." He assessed her briefly and looked away.

She twisted her head to see the photograph of Broussard's daughter once again. He was right. Both Vivian and the woman in the photograph had fair skin, blue eyes, and dark auburn hair. But as she stared at the girl, it was Molly who came to her mind.

"Time to go," Javier said when Edouard finished his speech and left the stage. The lights came back on, bright as before, and the band resumed playing.

Although several people surrounded him, they slowly made their way out of the ballroom. Javier didn't let her out of his sight for one moment, and she knew the intrusive bodyguard was around somewhere, watching her every step.

"Javier."

A deep female voice called to him.

Vivian glanced at Javier, who inhaled sharply before turning around to talk to an older woman. She wore a glamorous black dress with a long pearl necklace. Her heavy makeup seemed to carefully minimize all the years she had lived.

Silence descended upon them, lasting a moment longer than was socially acceptable. Javier's features hardened. If there was any emotion behind his blank stare, he hid it well.

The woman finally spoke. "It's nice to see you."

"I didn't know you'd be here," Javier said.

"I came for the party. I will go back to Madrid tonight. How have you been?" She took one step forward, her sad black eyes searching for his.

"Good," he answered. His fingers clenched at Vivian's waist, the gesture telling her that something about this woman unsettled him. He could not show it or say it, but she felt the tension in his body. It prompted her to stretch her hand out to the woman and say, "I'm Vivian Foster. Nice to meet you."

The woman blinked, slightly taken aback. With the hint of a smile, she shook Vivian's hand. "I'm Gisela Rivera. Javier's mother."

His mother. Of course. They shared the same dark eyes and full lips, but the similarities ended there.

Vivian sensed that Gisela longed for a deeper connection to her son—which made her wonder, how could such an important relationship be allowed to degenerate to the extent that Javier and his mother could have this awkward run-in?

"I sent you an invitation for the family reunion in November," Gisela said.

"I've been busy." Javier inhaled. After another long pause, he said, "Good night."

His mother simply nodded, as if she not only expected this kind of treatment from him but accepted it.

Vivian shot Javier's mother a sympathetic smile over her shoulder as Javier's hand on her back prompted her to match his decisive strides out of the ballroom.

Chapter Four

Vivian leaned against the cold wall of the elevator and sighed as she glanced at their reflection in the mirrored walls.

They were all alone. Javier stood straight and faced forward with his features set in hard lines, waiting for the doors to open. She sagged against the wall, her gaze alternating between the mirror and his broad back and strong shoulders.

The oppressive silence didn't seem to faze him. When the doors opened, Javier walked out of the elevator and into the hallway with his usual confidence. Vivian wished she could see his eyes, although she knew deep down it wasn't a smart impulse. Whatever flickers of emotion he tried to hide from his mother were not her problem.

I don't care how he got this way. I don't. Vivian chanted the mantra inside her head.

She had other things to think about. Since she had talked—damn it, she had *danced*—with Monsieur Broussard himself, hope had blossomed inside her. A part of her knew Edouard would at least look into her accusation, just as she knew Molly hadn't committed suicide. Call it intuition or instinct—whatever it was, she trusted it. She had made progress.

The knowledge should have brought her some comfort. It should not have been clashing with growing doubts.

But it was.

"What are you looking at?" Javier asked, arching an eyebrow.

"Your scar," she blurted out. "Did you get hurt at cricket?"

"No." A curt reply.

"Rugby?"

Certainly a man like Javier, born and bred into the upper crust of Spanish society, had not been scarred doing something noble. A sports injury was the most likely scenario.

"It was a fight," he said tightly.

"How sophisticated."

"I was eight."

Vivian stopped short. *Eight.* "Was the other child hurt, as well?"

"It wasn't a child. It was my stepfather, back in Spain." He almost sounded casual, but she noticed the tension in his jaw and the careful way he pronounced the words, as if each one of them carried a heavy weight.

"I'm sorry." Vivian bit down on her lip so hard, she could taste the blood inside her mouth. Her first impulse was to touch him, to comfort him, but she pulled back her hand before it was too late.

She couldn't hug him. This was the man who put her best friend through hell. This was the man who had handcuffed her last night.

"You didn't know rich kids get beaten, too?" He sounded angry, but before she could respond, he spoke again, and this time he'd removed all the emotion from his voice. "It was a long time ago."

The pain that remained in his eyes told her that the real

scar was rooted deep inside his soul.

She chastised herself silently. *You have no business being anywhere near his soul.*

But still, she wondered. Did it happen often? Did his mother know?

He strolled in the direction of the suite, motioning to her to do the same. Vivian went along, although her heart resisted following his orders, even as her legs obeyed.

She had to say something. She couldn't give him a hug, nor could she use his troubled past to justify his actions. But for reasons she couldn't understand, she just couldn't drop the subject. "Despite what you may think, I really am—"

"Don't." His warning glance told her this was none of her business.

Vivian nodded. Who was she to push a subject he'd probably only brought up to make her feel bad? Yet the unbearable silence made her more aware of her pounding heart and sweating palms. To escape the torturous thoughts that threatened to cloud her judgment, she asked, "What's on the agenda for tomorrow?"

"Since my bodyguard can't resist your charms, tomorrow I won't let you out of my sight."

"If you want something done, do it yourself?" she asked as he opened the door to their suite. Vivian looked at the hallway one last time, staring at the elegant striped wallpaper and the Louis XIV chairs located at the far end of the hall, close to the elevator. She saw the shadow of the bodyguard coming toward them and knew he would guard her room even at night.

There's no way out, is there?

"After being cuffed, hostage to a spa day, and then forced to dance with you at the ball, I must say I'm worried about what else you can do to me." Vivian had meant to say it playfully, to relax the elevated tension between them. But a nervous chuckle followed the words, and Javier cocked his head.

"I can do a lot more." His husky voice sent a chill chasing down her spine.

She gripped the skirt of her dress with shaking fingers, lifting it slightly so she could get to her room more quickly. She could feel his eyes on her, and she became aware it wasn't just his gaze—he was walking dangerously close behind her.

She stopped in front of her door and turned around to look at him. His door was across from hers, but the way he stood beside her, his eyes burning into hers as he leaned close, Javier didn't look as if he was about to go to his room.

Will he sleep with me—in my bed—again? No, no, no.

"What's wrong, Vivian?"

"Nothing," she said, and her eyes rose to meet his. As their gazes locked, a surge of desire ripped through her, challenging her common sense.

His index finger outlined her jaw, holding her chin up, his touch a whisper of what was to come…

Vivian wanted to move.

I should move.

I have to move.

Yet the blissful warmth of his fingers held her captive for a few more seconds, and the back of his hand touched her cheek with a tenderness that almost undid her. With her eyes half closed, Vivian let a tortured sigh escape her open lips. She backed away from his touch before her last thread of rationality could slip away.

"I have to…" She cleared her throat, reaching behind her for the door handle.

All she needed was the strength to turn it.

She would turn the door handle, say good night, and go to bed. All alone.

"Yes, you do." Javier leaned over her, positioning his right hand to open the door for her. "We both do."

His body moved into hers, the warmth of his thighs pushing her back against the door. His lips hovered over hers.

Vivian immediately spread both hands over his broad chest, her rational mind at war with a raw, fierce desire unfamiliar to her. She had never experienced anything like it before. She pushed at him, trying to resist the feelings overtaking her, but his hard, powerful body made it impossible. All remaining doubt disappeared, and her pushing turned into pulling. Obeying a violent urge, she drew him closer and parted her lips, and his hot tongue slipped inside her mouth to begin a tormenting search, exploring every corner.

Vivian's knees quivered, and he held her steady while his free hand angled the back of her head so his mouth could prolong the sweet agony. Her nipples hardened, peaking against the lace of her bra. Her quick response to him astonished her.

For a brief moment, he tore his mouth from hers. A moan of protest escaped her lips, and he kissed her chin, letting his lips slide down her neck, tasting her skin with his tongue. She threw her head back and pulled him closer as she ran her fingers through his short hair. Then he claimed her mouth again, branding her with a heat that spread in her body like flames on dry tinder. Never before she had been kissed with such passion. Never before had she been so aroused. Never before in her life had a kiss turned her into a rag doll or filled her with such reckless abandon.

"Tell me, Vivian…" He withdrew his mouth, his forehead touching hers as his own breathing heaved.

"Yes," she whispered. *Yes, yes, yes…*

"Do you believe me now?"

At first, his meaning didn't register. Her mind raced, her body burning with a profusion of needs awakened by Javier's touch.

"Tell me you do," he demanded, straightening his shoulders and moving back a little.

Vivian took a few seconds to understand what he was saying, returning to awareness as if she were just waking up from the effects of an anesthetic.

The passionate man who had just kissed her sanity away had been replaced by the cold, money-driven tycoon.

Then she understood.

He wanted compliance—he'd just changed his tactics. Or maybe he was paying her back for crashing his party without an invitation. Either way, while his kiss had destroyed her reason, for him it had been a tool of manipulation.

What a gullible fool she was.

Vivian snapped out of her lethargy. Driven by a different kind of heat, she slapped him hard enough to make her hand sting.

He pressed his hand to his cheek with an expression that hinted at his surprise at her boldness. Or perhaps her foolishness.

She didn't care what he thought. She hoped that for a man like Javier, being slapped by a woman would damage his ego, even if it couldn't damage him physically.

"Have a good night, Javier."

She yanked the door open and locked it behind her, then leaned back against it, her chest heavy and laden with the burden of regret.

What have I done?

Vivian touched her lips, still burning from his kiss, and knew exactly what she had done. She had lost herself in the arms of the enemy, and she had come far too close to betraying her mission. Not to mention her common sense, which had vanished into thin air the moment he touched her.

She walked shakily to the beige chair in front of the vanity mirror and clung to the wooden dresser for balance. A quick glance at her reflection revealed flushed cheeks and swollen lips, reminding her that no man in her past had ever made her feel like this.

It was ironic that the first time she experienced such a strong attraction, it was for a man who was not worth it. The man who had broken Molly's heart and —

"Molly."

Vivian covered her mouth with her hand. A hot tear rolled down her cheek.

I have to be strong. I can't fall into the same trap Molly did.

Every waking second I spend with him, I have to remember what happened to Molly.

The strong sunlight straying inside the bedroom warned Vivian that it was well past seven o'clock. She yawned, rubbing her fingers across eyes that were gritty after a night of tossing and turning. With a deep sigh, she swung her legs over the side of the bed just as she heard a knock on the door.

She slipped a thick, white robe over her nightgown before opening the door to the female room service attendant, who strolled inside with a heavily laden breakfast cart.

"*Bonjour,* Mademoiselle Foster." Vivian noticed a different bodyguard standing in front of her room. This one was bald and stocky, and as he held the door open, she noticed his stern expression. "You will find all you need here, Mademoiselle." The attendant's friendly tone was at odds with the exaggerated lift of her eyebrows. "I hope the tea will be to your liking."

Vivian smiled and looked down the tray. The tip of an envelope peeked out from beneath the teapot. "I'll try it, thank you."

She closed the door behind the attendant, anxious to see

what was in the envelope. There was nothing written on the outside. Inside, she found a folded note containing a single phone number.

A knock sounded on the door, making her jump. She quickly folded the slip of paper and hid it in a bedside drawer.

She opened the door, her throat dry. "Javier."

He'd dressed casually, but he was just as attractive as he'd been in a formal suit. The short-sleeved white button-up shirt fitted snugly over his chest, exposing his strong arms and enhancing his golden coloring.

"Good morning, Vivian," he said casually. "Did you sleep well?" He seemed to have forgotten that they had parted on less than amicable terms.

"Never better." Folding her arms, Vivian raised her chin, looking into his black eyes.

She had tried and failed to forget that kiss. Instead, it had replayed in her memory many times throughout the night. Now, with Javier close to her once more, his hair damp from the shower and the scent of a clean soap on his warm skin, she had to acknowledge that any attempt to forget about the kiss would be futile.

"About the kiss," he said, as though reading her thoughts.

"You mean my lapse in judgment? It's long forgotten."

"I've been playing it in my head, over and over."

"It doesn't matter," Vivian said, her heart thumping in her chest. "You lied, though. When we danced, you made me believe you wouldn't try for any sort of…involvement with me."

"I told you it was no problem if you weren't attracted to me." He smiled. "I never said I wasn't attracted to you."

"Oh, please. Your attraction to me had nothing to do with that kiss."

"The kiss again… I thought it was forgotten." He closed the distance between them, but she stepped back, clutching both sides of her robe together.

"It is. Forgotten, I mean."

He sighed and looked past her to her untouched breakfast cart. "I see you haven't had breakfast yet. Come with me."

"What about the food? It would be a shame to let it go to waste."

"It won't. Nelson, the bodyguard, is quite fond of pastries."

She imagined the bodyguard feasting on the sugar-coated pastries and couldn't suppress a chuckle. Once she'd sobered, she said, "I have to get ready. Can we skip the limo? I'd rather walk." Vivian didn't know how yet, but she was going to find a way to call the new number Roger had given her. She had to tell him about the progress she'd made the previous night. She didn't want to be limited to the inside of a limousine—and, if she was being honest with herself, she didn't want to be in an enclosed space with Javier beside her.

"You have thirty minutes."

Vivian closed the door behind him. She had to get creative, and fast…

Javier looked at the message from his private investigator on the screen of his phone.

No ties between Foster and your opponents yet. I'll text with updates.

Perhaps she wasn't allied with his enemies—perhaps her interest in him really was all about Molly Richardson. But doubt haunted his thoughts. Could the person she had called from the restaurant be merely a friend or a lover? She'd had the Webb proposal when he'd found her in his office, and that was a small deal. Last night, she hadn't even known who Edouard Broussard was.

According to his investigator, she had worked in an art

gallery before applying for the receptionist position. She didn't have any family in the country. Her only blood relative was an aunt who lived in the United States and who had claimed not to know much about her niece.

Javier cursed silently. No one seemed to know anything about the woman he'd taken custody of.

He wanted to learn more about her. He knew he couldn't trust her, but this knowledge didn't prevent a part of him from wondering what would have happened if he hadn't broken that kiss.

The most erotic experience he'd ever had with his clothes on. The moment their tongues had swirled together, Vivian had surpassed any fantasy. She had been an active partner, matching his need, his passion, stroke for stroke. Yes, it was easy to imagine what it would be like to make love to her.

They would have had a long night of passion, giving in to the desire that threatened his usual self-control. Images of Vivian in his bed, her naked body under his, her blue eyes darkening with pleasure, had tortured him through a sleepless night.

One way or another, he had to do something about this. Javier tucked his phone in his pocket and headed to her room. When he got no response to three firm knocks, he pushed the door open and strode in. The room was empty.

"Vivian?"

He found her facing the Eiffel Tower. Javier stepped closer until he was behind her, breathing in her scent, the note of lavender inebriating his senses. The mild spring breeze played with the ends of her loose hair. He closed his fists, tightening his fingers until his knuckles whitened.

Vivian broke the silence. "Beautiful, isn't it?"

"Gorgeous." He glanced at her profile, still and focused on the city awakening before her.

A black pencil skirt molded her hips, and a white

cashmere sweater fit snugly across her breasts. His hand fell to the indentation of her waist, and she moved to the side, away from his touch.

Javier let out a breath in frustration. "Avoiding this insane attraction won't make it go away."

"I'll give it a try." She crossed her arms and looked out at the city.

"It won't work," he insisted. His fingers sizzled when he touched her arm and turned her to face him.

"We'll make it work." She spoke with confidence, but her blue eyes revealed her uncertainty.

"Reason won't have much power over this." His index finger trailed down her neck, and he smiled when he felt the mad beat of her pulse at the base of her throat. She could deny and lie all she wanted, but her body told him the truth.

She was wrong for him, but her body, her skin felt so right.

"Is that what you tell all your lovers to get them into bed?" She pulled away from him, a delicate flush on her cheeks.

"I never have to." It was the truth. Women were usually drawn to him like bees to honey. Not that he complained, but over the years he had become a lot more selective about his female companions.

She rolled her eyes. "There's a first time for everything, isn't there?"

"I've had plenty of firsts lately." He shook his head.

"How so?" Her polished fingernails caressed the metal rail of the balcony. He imagined those soft hands cupping his shaft, her delicate fingers tracing along his length.

Javier cleared his throat. "The first time I slept next to a woman without having sex. The first time I kissed someone as passionately as we did without going further."

"I'm not your new toy," she warned him, concern flashing in her eyes.

"No, you're not. That's why I'm about to take you out for

an innocent Sunday breakfast."

"Another first?"

He nodded. "Let's go."

Chapter Five

The Café Toujours was located in a prime area, famous for its view overlooking the sun-dappled Seine river and for the eclectic crowd of bohemian locals, intellectuals, and trendsetters. Vivian sipped her orange juice as she sat opposite Javier on the terrace outside the café.

It was a beautiful morning. She squinted toward the river, trying to exhale the tension from her shoulders.

"Why aren't you comfortable with your height?" Javier asked.

"Pardon?"

"I noticed you wore flats the first day I saw you. You tend to slightly hunch instead of walking tall."

Vivian straightened her shoulders. "I don't hunch."

"You almost tripped last night."

"I'm not a professional dancer," she retorted.

"I meant when you were walking in high heels."

"Suddenly I'm the hunchback of Notre-Dame?"

His warm laugh was as intimate as a caress. "Not quite like the hunchback. But why?"

"I don't..." She sighed, too tired to be combative. A moment later, she said, "It was my father."

"Your bad posture is hereditary?" he teased.

"No." She cleared her throat. "Well, I don't know. He left when I was four."

She wondered whether to say more. Vivian wasn't keen on sharing her emotions with strangers—let alone enemies—but life was so uncertain that Javier might be the last person she'd tell this to. What if he threw her in jail after finding out her plan to take the merger away from him?

"After a few years, my mom remarried. My stepfather was a nice man. She was petite, he was barely average height. I always felt different, being so tall like my biological father. I wanted to blend." The throaty rasp in her voice gave away how distressing she still found the memory.

"You thought shrinking your shoulders would help," Javier said.

"It's not something I do consciously. I guess every time we were on family outings or when I looked at pictures of us, my biological father leaving me would be at the back of my mind. I was hurt by him never even wanting to get to know me. He never gave me a chance."

"Did you look for him as an adult?"

She nodded. "After my mom and stepfather died, I looked. But he still didn't want anything to do with me."

And she'd felt so guilty for looking after having promised her mother she wouldn't. The whole thing had been a fiasco.

Vivian closed her eyes, feeling the lump in her throat slowly dissolve. She didn't know if her relief arose from sharing a crucial part of what made her what she was, or simply because she felt at ease telling him the truth.

"Vivian."

Javier spoke gently, and as she opened her eyes, a hot tear rolled down her cheek. She wiped it off with the back of her hand.

Remember why you're here. Remember.

"It's all right, really. My stepfather was a loving parent."

"Not everyone is that lucky," Javier said.

"You're right." She looked at his scar. "Did your mom know?"

"She thought I was a difficult child. I grew up thinking he was my father, never understanding why he treated me like a second-class citizen." There was a terrible sadness in his voice.

"How did you find out he wasn't your father?"

"One day, I overheard a conversation between him and my mother, and it all made sense." His fingers played with the rim of his coffee cup. His relaxed posture couldn't conceal the pain she saw sparking in his eyes.

"How long had he known it?"

"He suspected it for a while, then pressured my mother for a paternity test when I was four."

"What about your biological father?"

"My mother had an affair with a poor man, according to her. When she found out she was pregnant, she broke off the affair without telling him about the pregnancy. Instead, she used it as bait for her then-fiancé, my stepfather, to set the wedding date and marry her."

"I'm sorry. That's just wrong."

"That's life." He shot her an unconvincing smile.

"Did you ever look for your real father?"

"Yes, but it was too late. He died as an ordinary man, without ever knowing he had a wealthy son."

"He would have liked to know he had a son, period."

"We'll never know." He shrugged.

Without thinking, she moved her fingers over the table to cover his hand, but the waiter appeared with their orders, and she stopped herself.

Javier sipped an espresso and ate a pastry, his fingers

touching his jeans pocket from time to time as if he was waiting for his phone to ring.

As if their conversation had never taken place.

Chillness engulfed her. It was unsettling how he could switch from real person to distant businessman at the drop of a hat. She could tell he didn't share that story with a lot of people. It was difficult for him to talk about his childhood. Being abused by his mother's husband must have shaped him into the man he was today.

And what kind of man is he?

The more she knew about him, the more complicated everything became.

"We have some time to kill," Javier said with a breezy smile. "How about another first—we can visit an overcrowded landmark. The Eiffel Tower? Sacré-Coeur?"

Vivian couldn't help smiling. "How about the Louvre?"

"The Louvre it is."

"Okay. Can we stop by a souvenir shop first?" He frowned, and she explained, "I'm entitled to have my 'I Love Paris' shirt."

"I thought you wouldn't want any memory of being here against your will."

"A souvenir will make me appreciate life more once I'm back."

"There's a store not too far from here."

"Good," she said. They left the café and strolled along the pavement. Vivian spotted the bodyguard following them at a distance that was short enough for him to catch up quickly if he needed to, yet distant enough for them to forget about his presence—a reminder that although they had shared painful childhood memories, Javier still didn't trust her on her own.

And considering what she was about to do, that was probably wise.

"Which one do you like better?" Vivian feigned indecision and for the third time showed Javier two very similar magnets.

"This one." He pointed at the left one, visibly annoyed. They were inside a crowded souvenir shop, and she was torturing him.

"Really?" She looked at the one he'd picked and made a face. She was about to select a couple of other souvenirs when his phone rang.

"I need to take this," he said.

"I need cash. You took my wallet." He handed her a couple of large bills before moving a few feet away from her to take his call.

With Javier busy on the phone she stood in line to pay, smiling to herself. There were a couple of tourists chatting happily in front of her, but if the cashier worked fast enough, she would get what she wanted. She randomly picked out a shirt, magnets, and some of the pens that overflowed from bins close to the register. What she needed most was displayed on the wall behind the counter.

She glanced over her shoulder and saw Javier focused on his call. The bodyguard was outside, his back turned to the window glass. "I'm going to need one of your prepaid mobiles," she told the cashier. "Please be discreet and wrap it with the shirt."

The cashier retrieved a phone from behind him. "It comes with fifty minutes of prepaid talk time, and if you look inside, there's a number."

"That's fine. Just pack it up, okay? I'm in a hurry."

The cashier nodded. As he was placing the last items into a plastic bag, Javier returned.

"Are you done?" he asked.

"Yes," she said with a smile. "I have everything I need."

As they stepped out of the souvenir shop, it began to rain.

"We need a cab." Javier stretched out his hand, and after a brief hesitation she accepted it.

The traffic was chaotic. She didn't see any available cabs, and soon thick raindrops replaced the initial drizzle. Pedestrians sought shelter inside cafés or headed toward their parked vehicles.

Vivian blinked, glancing toward the unexpected dark cloud in an otherwise clear sky. Her white cashmere sweater clung to her like a second skin. She looked down at her soaked clothes, suppressing a chuckle. She couldn't remember the last time she'd gotten soaked in the rain. Her hardened nipples were visible through her white lace bra and dampened sweater. When she lifted her eyes, she found that Javier, too, was looking, and she felt a wave of heat flush her cheeks.

With wet hair and raindrops rolling down his face, Javier looked undeniably male.

"*Venga*." He pulled her a couple of steps off the street, pressing her against a wall beneath a narrow, dripping awning.

Vivian found herself sandwiched between damp, cold brick and Javier, who was not fully sheltered from the raindrops, though he didn't seem to mind.

A diabolical smile spread across his face, and a knot rose in her throat.

His grin disappeared as he leaned down to touch his full lips to her parted mouth. As soon as the kiss began, his urgent, hot tongue intertwined with hers. An ache grew between her legs. She felt a hard bulge against her thigh. Their clothes became a loathsome nuisance.

A current of need shook her from head to toe. Vivian moaned when he withdrew his lips from hers for a brief, painful moment. He murmured in coarse Spanish, and she imagined him making erotic promises of all the ardent things he wanted to do with her…for her…to her.

With her pulse pounding, she nibbled on the sexiest male lips she'd ever tasted. She wondered, for a moment, how they would feel on her…

And then, as suddenly as the summer storm, a faraway police siren broke the spell, and Vivian thought, *I will regret this*.

Shaking her head, she attempted to move away from Javier, but her slight sway molded their bodies into a more perfect fit. She widened her eyes.

"I—I can't do this," she gasped. "I have to get out of these clothes."

"My thoughts exactly." He rubbed his fingertip against her hard nipple, her thin, soaked clothing barely a barrier between his warm finger and the erect bud.

"I mean I can't do this. Us, being intimate. I have to go back to the hotel to change out of these wet clothes."

"Why can't you?" he asked, without loosening his grip on her.

She paused and then sighed. "Because it will only make what I have to do harder." She pushed him away enough that she could think more clearly. "Because you slept with Molly, Javier."

"Several months ago, when you were not in the picture." He rubbed the back of his neck with his hand and sighed. "If she were alive today, I'm sure she would have moved on."

She couldn't disagree. Molly had been too vibrant to suffer over any man for long.

But wasn't that the point? *This* man had made Molly suffer.

He'd done worse than that. He'd ended her life.

Maybe.

"Stop thinking for a moment," he said. "Let's go to the

hotel and have all the sex we need to get this out of our systems."

His words brought her back to reality.

"Sex. Of course," Vivian said, upset at the disappointment in her tone.

If there were no Molly, no two-faced Javier, no kidnapping of her to Paris…if their surroundings were completely different and he was just a man and she was just a woman… Even then, this would never work.

A cold chill rushed through her veins as he spoke softly. "I want you very much, Vivian. I know you feel the same."

She closed her eyes, massaging her temples. How could she deny it after practically mauling him in public? She glanced around, but they were alone. Well, not quite. The bodyguard still hovered at a safe distance.

"Is it because of the circumstances?"

"No. Even if things were different… I'm not like you, Javier. I'm not sophisticated, and I don't have sex with people I barely know and move on." She spoke with a quiet dignity. Damn him, it was hard enough moving away from him literally, to disentangle her limbs from his, to dismiss his kiss… She could not imagine how catastrophic it would be for any woman to climb out of his bed after a night of passionate lovemaking.

I'll never know. I won't ever be that woman.

"That's how you see it." He cursed in Spanish under his breath.

"I can't stop thinking. I'm sorry."

Stopping thinking is a luxury I can't afford.

"We'll change our clothes at the hotel," he said. "Separately." She heard his frustration in the way he pronounced the word. "And then we'll visit the Louvre."

"Thank you," she whispered.

They hailed a cab and returned to the hotel, and to her relief Javier didn't make her feel awkward about what had occurred between them. Once alone in her room, Vivian tossed the plastic bag on the bed and got out of her wet clothes, changing quickly into a sand-colored wool dress.

She set up the prepaid mobile and called the number on the piece of paper.

"It's Vivian," she said when the other person picked up after the first ring.

"I'm glad to hear your voice at last. What do you have for me?" Roger asked.

"Yesterday, we went to Mr. Broussard's charity fund-raiser. But I didn't know who he was until the end. Mr. Broussard, that is." Vivian cupped one hand over the mobile to keep the sound of her voice from carrying. "I was able to ask him to look into Molly's death."

"Good girl. What else did you tell him?"

"I didn't have much time." She looked at the door to make sure she was still alone.

"Don't back down, Vivian. Rivera got off easy, paying for Molly's funeral expenses and walking away." Roger's tone was terse.

"What do you mean? You told me her mother was stuck with the expenses."

"I thought so, too. But afterward I found out he paid for the funeral."

Something about that didn't make sense. "Why would Javier pay for the funeral if he was trying to buy her silence? Why wouldn't he offer her a lot of money to keep her from causing a scandal?"

"He probably fooled the poor woman somehow, got her to accept even less than she deserved. But since when is he

'Javier' to you?"

"He isn't." She chewed on her lower lip. "I've confronted him about killing Molly, and he denied it. He didn't deny that he slept with her or that he left her an angry voice mail."

"And you believed him?"

"What if the investigator he hired had something to do with it?"

"The investigator?" Roger laughed. "Vivian, don't be ridiculous." When he spoke again, his tone had sobered. "Don't lose sight of what you're there for. That's not what Molly would have wanted."

The urge to reply burned at the tip of her tongue. Who has he to talk about what Molly would have wanted?

"I'll be in touch soon," he said.

Vivian ended the call. She'd barely had time to dry her hair when she heard the knock on her door. Javier appeared, looking as handsome as ever in dark trousers and a short-sleeved light gray polo shirt. Memories of his touch on her skin, his tongue in her mouth both troubled and exhilarated her.

The heavy load of guilt kept her in check. She couldn't allow herself to indulge her attraction to the man who may have taken her best friend's life.

She couldn't, and she wouldn't.

"You like museums?" Javier asked as they entered the European paintings department of the Louvre.

"The Louvre isn't a museum. It's more like a parallel universe." Vivian stared in awe at the masterpieces on the wall. This was heaven for anyone who enjoyed the arts, and in a different situation she would be much more at ease. But it was getting harder and harder to relax—or to pretend she wasn't in utter turmoil inside — when he was around.

"Beauty and brains. Why doesn't the man you called from the restaurant see that?"

She continued looking through the museum directory, her fingers playing with the flyer. "What makes you say that?" she asked.

"What kind of man sends his lover off to the lion's den?" When she raised her eyes to meet his, the little hairs on the back of her neck stood up. His gaze pinned hers, and she felt trapped.

If he's the lion, what am I? Dinner?

"It's not what you think."

"Educate me." Javier crossed his arms.

For a moment, she wished she could. Her conversation with Roger had left her with a nagging feeling that wouldn't go away. Something didn't add up. After Molly's funeral, Vivian hadn't had time to talk to Molly's mother, Laura. She was a reserved woman, distant. Vivian had never felt a connection to her, and Molly and Laura weren't close. But Laura hadn't deserved to lose her daughter.

Vivian had felt such sympathy for Laura, forced to cope with her daughter's death and to pay the unexpected costs of the funeral. Roger had played on that sympathy — and now it seemed he'd been lying to her.

What else might he have lied about?

But the facts remained. Molly had fallen for Javier. He'd broken it off, left her a threatening message, and then Molly had ended up dead. Vivian couldn't believe Molly would have killed herself.

She couldn't believe Javier was an innocent party in what had happened to her best friend.

Vivian swallowed the stubborn lump in her throat. "The French paintings are up ahead."

A couple minutes later, she was drawn to the famous

painting of Napoleon crowning Josephine, and she viewed the huge oil canvas on the dark red wall with a sad smile. There it was in all its glory in front of her—rich colors, precise details. The blushing woman receiving the title of empress as a man held up the crown, high and proud, before the gathered monarchs.

She looked over her shoulder and saw Javier checking his phone.

The painting drew her back. Josephine had been dishonest to Napoleon before starting to love him. And when she had finally been ready for honesty, it was too late. Once Napoleon found out about the way she'd misbehaved in Paris while he was away at war, his feelings for her changed. Later, they divorced.

Relationships based on lies never survived.

"She betrayed him," Javier said from behind her, a touch of bitterness in his voice.

"Maybe at first, but at the end it was different."

"The end is never different." His voice was cold.

"Is that one of the mottos you live by?" Vivian glanced at him over her shoulder. "That all women are the same? That must make it easy when you break their hearts." *Or worse.*

"I don't think they're all the same. Take you, for instance, Vivian Foster." He spoke her name with a drawl, long and drawn-out, as if it were some difficult mathematical equation. "I'm not sure I've ever met anyone quite like you."

"Why is that?"

He stepped forward, and although the spacious section where they stood was virtually empty, she felt as though the whole room had filled with his presence.

"That's what I want to find out."

"Javier...is there any chance your investigator hired the men to follow Molly?" she asked. "Do you know him well?" *Do you know what he's capable of?*

"I've used him a couple of times in the past, when I needed background information on high-profile business associates. I doubt he would do such thing. His name is Matt Smith."

"Where was he when she died?" Vivian asked.

"Eating noodle soup," he said sarcastically. "Watching television. With a woman. I don't know, Vivian."

She parted her lips to respond—and then hesitated. She had to consider all the possibilities. Molly had been very attractive. What if this Matt fellow had been involved with Molly, or had wanted to be? What if he'd become obsessed with her? There were all sorts of lunatics in the world.

She stared at the painting in silence.

Javier's phone rang, and he stepped away to take the call.

Javier glanced at the caller ID and shook his head. He'd been waiting for Matt to call him back with more information, but no luck.

"Hello?"

"Javier, hello." Edouard greeted him. "I'm calling to ask you about your friend, Vivian. I wondered if she'd be available to join us for dinner tonight."

Javier's blood pounded thick in his veins. *He's calling me to ask Vivian out?*

Had it been any man other than Edouard, his answer would have been far less diplomatic. However, he was less than a day away from signing the merger, and with that in mind, he managed to say lightly, "I'm afraid she already has plans."

"Oh, but I meant for all of us to have dinner. Mind you, I will have some company myself." The Frenchman chuckled.

"Perhaps we can arrange something for next week?" Javier suggested.

By next week, he would have his merger complete, and what Vivian thought of him would no longer matter. By then, he would either have found out more about her or convinced her he hadn't killed Molly. His chest tightened.

Vivian would no longer be his concern. Why did the thought bring him no relief?

"But it would be a great opportunity for us to meet one more time before the big signing tomorrow. It will of course be an intimate gathering, not a business affair. I just need your strong presence to give this old man peace of mind before signing my life away tomorrow."

It didn't take a genius to read between the lines. Javier's presence was mandatory—and so was Vivian's.

He breathed out carefully, rubbing his hand over his forehead.

Vivian looked as still as a statue in front of the painting.

She hadn't known who Edouard was when they danced. There was no connection between her and the Broussard merger. And apparently Edouard would be busy with a companion of his own.

This could hardly be a trap. But Javier didn't trust it.

"We'll cancel our plans for tonight and meet you for dinner," he said.

"Wonderful. I will wait for you at my house, at seven."

He hung up the phone and walked over to Vivian. "We have dinner plans."

Chapter Six

Vivian looked out the window as the limousine made its way through tall wrought iron gates and passed by a seemingly endless stretch of manicured gardens and century-old trees.

All through the drive to the elegant mansion on the outskirts of Paris, she had alternated among shifting in her seat, crossing and uncrossing her legs, and running her fingers nervously through her loose hair. She looked across at Javier. He wore black pants and a black shirt, which enhanced the color of his eyes and his deep olive skin.

Had Edouard called him—summoned them to this dinner—to tell Javier what she had said? What would happen?

"Interesting how he remembered you," Javier said. "He even remembered your name. Why?"

Vivian straightened her shoulders. "If you must know, he told me I resemble his daughter."

"You are saying he's not interested in you?"

"I'm confident he's not interested in me the way you think."

"In the way that I am," he challenged, spacing out the

words. His eyes swept over her figure, and his lips turned upward in a slow, indecent smile.

"Most definitely in no such way." She managed to say it matter-of-factly, wrapping her black scarf around her neck and wishing she'd worn something with more coverage than the dark red halter dress with a V neckline.

The limousine parked at the entrance of a luxurious house. "We're here," she said.

A tall man dressed in a butler's uniform opened the door before they even rang the bell and ushered them into the living room.

Edouard appeared behind the butler, smiling. "Javier. Vivian. How nice to see you both."

Javier and Edouard shared an amicable handshake, and then the old man greeted Vivian with a smile and a kiss on both cheeks. "I appreciate you two indulging this older man for some company." He signaled for them to sit on the L-shaped sofa.

"Thank you for having us. Your place is quite beautiful." Vivian's eyes took in the hardwood floors, the Persian rugs, the oversized fireplace, and the imperial art pieces hanging on the beige stone walls. His house was luxurious and tastefully decorated.

The butler reappeared with a bottle of wine and a beautiful crystal tray of cheeses, pâtés, caviars, and pastries. As he poured wine in their flutes, the doorbell rang, and Edouard chose to open the door himself.

"I hope you don't mind, I've asked someone else join us," Edouard said as he walked to the hallway.

"Is that your companion for the evening?" Javier asked, sneaking his arm around Vivian's waist. His fingers tapped nervously against her side, and her dress proved no protection against the scorching sensation. His obviously possessive gesture left her confused. Did he still think she was somehow interested in a man old enough to be her father? And why would he care?

"She's a dear friend, and we both know her," Edouard answered casually. He greeted the newcomer and brought her into the living room. "Dominique, I am so pleased you could join us."

Vivian turned her head to see a petite blond woman wearing a dark pink dress that complemented every single curve. Dominique greeted Javier with delight, kissing both his cheeks and saying something in French with a teasing look. Javier didn't appear happy to see her. Then her eyes met Vivian's, and if for a moment the Frenchwoman was surprised, she hid it very well, offering a brief "hello" before continuing to bat her long eyelashes at Javier.

Vivian had no idea what to make of it. She looked at Edouard, who sent her an amused wink.

For the next hour, Vivian watched, her stomach in knots, as Javier kept his temper. Barely. He responded with sympathy to Edouard, smoothly avoided Dominique's advances, and often rested his eyes on Vivian, tracking her every move.

Why did he dislike Dominique so much? Was she his lover or a former lover he didn't want Vivian to meet? Vivian looked across the table at her. Of course, she *had* to be petite and slim, with blond hair that cascaded down her shoulders.

She also had a shrewd awareness to her. This woman was no blond bimbo, Vivian was certain of that.

"So, Vivienne…" Dominique said after they'd been seated for dinner.

"It's Vivian."

"*Mais oui*…Vivian. You and Javier are business-related, I gather?"

"Vivian is someone who's made it impossible for me not to want to know more about her," Javier said.

Vivian was grateful for the rescue, although she didn't

feel the least bit safe with his dark eyes raking over her.

"There you go." Vivian turned to Dominique. "Are you and Edouard longtime acquaintances?"

"I'm remodeling his house in Saint-Tropez. I've also remodeled Javier's penthouse in Monaco." Dominique looked at Javier, who simply nodded. "And what do *you* do, Vivian?"

"Most of the time, I do as I please," Vivian replied. She knew the woman would laugh if she mentioned she worked as a receptionist, and she didn't want to give her the satisfaction.

Javier bestowed Vivian with an admiring smile.

For the rest of dinner, Javier paid little attention to Dominique, and Dominique became increasingly upset. Edouard smoothed the atmosphere with light jokes and good-spirited comments. After dinner, they returned to the living room for coffee and dessert wine.

Dominique cornered Javier near a large window, talking to him quietly in French. She appeared to be angry. Vivian was now certain the French woman had had an affair with Javier and that it had ended badly—at least for Dominique. She could tell by the woman's body language that she wanted another chance with Javier.

Shaking her head, she turned her attention to Edouard, who looked at her with amusement. He must have been watching her as she observed the interaction across the room.

Vivian looked down, feeling ashamed. She had reached a new low: speculating about Javier's love life. What a stupid waste of time…

I have to regroup.

She needed to splash some cold water on her face to cool her down and bring her to her senses.

"Where is the restroom?" Vivian asked.

"I'll show you, Mademoiselle Foster." The butler gestured for her to follow him, and as she walked from the room, she was aware of Javier's gaze fixed on her.

After using the facilities, she stepped into the wide hall, closing the bathroom door behind her. A sudden shadow in the hall startled her, making her gasp.

Edouard quickly stepped into the light. "Shh…" The older man approached her silently, finger to his lips. "I want to ask you about Molly Richardson."

Vivian nodded without speaking.

"I've tried calling you at the hotel, but it was impossible to contact you."

"So you came up with the dinner idea." Vivian smiled. The presence of Dominique now made complete sense. Edouard had invited one of Javier's former flames to make sure he'd be kept busy enough that Edouard could whisk her away for a talk.

"Yes. Vivian, I take requests seriously. People who are in trouble often have a hard time admitting it." His expression grew serious. "Are you in trouble, my dear?"

Vivian took a deep breath. "Molly Richardson was Javier's project manager in London. They had an affair that ended badly. She died two weeks afterward. The police ruled it a suicide, but I have my doubts."

Edouard grimaced.

"After the end of the affair, Molly was hurting. She tried to sabotage an important business deal by sharing information with an opponent. Javier couldn't afford any bad press. He fired her and tried to buy her off, but she refused to take his money." Vivian glanced behind Edouard to make sure they remained alone and unheard.

Edouard scratched his chin, his expression enigmatic.

"She told me a couple of men began to follow her every move. One day, she came home to find her flat turned upside down. Molly said one of the men manhandled her. She concluded that Javier had hired them to bully her into not selling any information she got her hands on." Vivian's voice trembled with emotion.

"Did she look for help?"

Vivian shook her head. "She said he threatened that if she went to the police, he would also sue her for having tried to sell insider information." Vivian could still hear Molly sobbing when she told the story.

"Who else knows about this?"

"She only told me about the whole thing after she couldn't take it anymore, shortly before her death. Maybe her mother knows, although they were estranged. And there's someone else involved—someone I can't tell you about. He knows it and may use it in his favor." Vivian clenched her hands, slippery with sweat.

This was what she had hoped for, wasn't it? To tell Edouard her story…so why didn't it feel like a victory?

"If this goes to the media, it won't be good for my foundation." Edouard sighed. "I will have this investigated. I have to be ready, in case anyone uses the press. I must find out the truth."

Vivian nodded.

"I must ask you, though…do you really believe Javier would kill someone and make it look like a suicide?"

Edouard's question hit her with the force of a thousand bricks. Not because it was unexpected, but because it was the question that had been nagging at her conscience. The question she'd been ignoring all day.

Did she really think Javier was a killer?

Did she really believe she was doing the right thing?

"I've brought it up to him, and he denied any wrongdoing. During the time I've spent with him, he hasn't done anything to hurt me." Vivian's voice wavered. She had to be fair to Javier, but she had to be fair to Molly, too. "But I knew Molly for fourteen years, and I swear she didn't kill herself. Maybe the man Javier hired to investigate Molly would have some more information. His name is Matt Smith." Vivian glanced at Edouard. His face showed concern, but she couldn't read anything else.

"This may sound crazy," she said, "but in the beginning I wanted to make Javier pay."

"And take away his merger?" Edouard concluded.

"I'm a horrible person, I know." She closed her eyes tightly.

"You are either a horrible person or a great friend." He smiled with compassion. "And I will find out soon."

"How?"

"I have my ways. I might have to delay my business transactions with him, though." He took a business card out of his pocket. "Call me if you need anything."

When Vivian rejoined the others a couple of minutes later, she could tell by Dominique's unpleasant expression that the Frenchwoman hadn't liked her chat with Javier at all.

Vivian sympathized. She hadn't enjoyed her chat with Edouard, either.

"Let's go for a walk," Javier said as the car cut through the streets of Paris.

It was the first time he'd spoken since leaving Edouard's mansion. He gave a quick order in French, and the driver stopped the limousine. Javier got out first, then helped her out. Her hand tingled where his fingers brushed against hers.

"Why do you want to walk?"

Vivian's high heels clicked on the concrete of the sidewalk along the Seine. It was dark, and the streets had emptied. She glanced at the river and thought of how many couples had shared kisses, declarations of love, or lover's tiffs on its bridges, on the sidewalks surrounding it, and on the cruise boats that navigated its waters.

"I'd rather do something else, but walking is safer," he said quietly.

Safer for whom?

Javier slowed down his pace and came to a full stop, prompting her to do the same. He leaned down just enough for her to hear him if he were to speak, but not enough so that his breath would whisper over her skin. Vivian held her own breath for as long as she could before inhaling in small gasps.

"Whatever else you had in mind," she said, "I'm sure Dominique would love to oblige."

He shook his head. "But I don't want Dominique."

His gaze slid over her, dropping to her lips and breasts. Vivian's nipples hardened, reacting to the command he silently gave. If he had said he wanted her, her reaction would be no less instantaneous.

"You slept with her, so she's no longer a novelty?"

The idea incensed her. Did he do that to all the women who crossed his path—seduce them relentlessly and then downgrade them to second-class citizenship when he was done with them?

She remembered Molly and had her answer.

"Dominique is not a victim. We had an arrangement. I hadn't seen her for months before tonight."

"You don't understand women, do you?"

"I understand women better than you think. It's you who I don't understand. Why are you defending Dominique when she would have been happy to claw you back there?"

"Because maybe she cared for you. Even with all your warning labels." As soon as the words made their way out of her mouth, she regretted saying them.

She wasn't talking about Dominique.

She wasn't even sure she was talking about Molly.

Although it was dark, she could still see the frown on his face. "You are a very loyal woman, Vivian." His cold voice chilled her. "Though you must be careful with such blind loyalty."

She swallowed. The silence deepened with every second that passed. His eyes locked on hers, and the small gap between them could have been as wide as the river.

He wasn't talking about Dominique, either.

"I only do what I think is right."

Vivian turned to face the river. It was so calm, it almost looked like a landscape painting.

"Look at me," he demanded.

She turned to face him. A warm glow outlined his black irises. The expression she found there was the same one he'd given her earlier, when they'd had breakfast and he'd told her about his painful childhood.

"I didn't kill her," he said. "I would never do such a thing."

He held her gaze. Her blurred thoughts began to take on a dangerous clarity. After spending every waking moment with him, after learning things about him that even he was not proud of…

"You didn't kill her?" Vivian asked.

He shook his head. And he never took his eyes off hers for a moment.

Those eyes weren't lying. *He* wasn't lying.

And damn it, she would be lying to herself if she pretended not to believe him.

She lifted her hand to her forehead, unsure what to think. Did his innocence bring her relief or more headaches? It complicated things a great deal. For just as she was sure he hadn't done it, she knew someone else had.

The man in front of her, whose eyes still rested on hers, stood as if awaiting her response.

She pressed her lips together hard, her emotions

thoroughly rattled. How could she give him the trust he wanted—the trust he'd *earned*—when she was a long way from understanding?

A couple of hours later, Javier gulped down a thirty-year-old scotch, pulled his shirt off, and kicked his shoes to the side.

The whiskey smoked its way down his throat, and he cursed himself.

When he'd slept with Molly, he hadn't expected to pay such a high price for it. He'd been tired and working too much, and he'd enjoyed the attention she'd poured over him at that stupid happy hour. It should have stopped there. He should have known better.

But he hadn't. He'd gone ahead and slept with an employee, something he'd vowed never to do—never to make his work vulnerable. Never to make himself vulnerable.

Then, after he'd found out her real intentions, he hated her. He'd felt used. Somehow that strong negative emotion lost its power when he found out she'd killed herself. What good was it to curse a tortured soul? He knew all about tortured souls.

And then there was Vivian—another woman who'd enticed him to make a mistake. But he couldn't shut off the part of his brain that insisted there was something else about her. Something important.

He would be signing the merger in less than ten hours, and it would put him right where he wanted to be. He should not be thinking of the woman who had denied him for the past couple of days.

But he couldn't stop.

She hadn't said one word after their exchange by the Seine. He'd expected her to protest fiercely, or at least to respond in some fashion. But her reaction had been a simple nod. Her expression had become remote, and she hadn't exchanged one more word with him.

He assumed she needed some time to come to terms with the fact that Molly had killed herself, and he looked forward to their conversation when she had reconciled herself almost more than he did to signing the merger.

Damn her for occupying his mind more than the merger.

Javier ran his fingers through his hair. He was about to undress and step into the shower when he heard her scream.

"No… Come back!"

Vivian.

Charging out of his room, he almost collided with the bodyguard, who was positioned to knock on his door. He elbowed him out of the way. "You can take a break. I'll deal with this. Leave us alone."

Her room was dark but for the light of the alarm clock on her bedside table. Javier closed the door behind him and approached her carefully. He turned the lamp on, brightening the area around her bed. Vivian was sitting up, slightly swaying and shaking her head.

Her white satin nightgown should have made her look serene, but the sweat on her forehead and darkening her temples gave her a more haunted look. She was having a nightmare again.

"Vivian, wake up," he said gently, but she didn't respond.

Javier shook her shoulders and spoke more firmly, "It's okay, Vivian. I am here."

That did it.

Her eyes flew open, filled with the expression of someone who had escaped one nightmare only to enter another. She looked around, her chest heaving, and her gaze locked with his. "What happened?"

"You had a nightmare."

She took a deep breath. "I'm sorry for waking you up."

He debated whether to ask what had scared her so much. A part of him wanted to know, and another part of him knew the best course of action would be to leave. The bubble of intimacy surrounding them was dangerous.

He reached out and removed a loose strand of hair from her face. He couldn't help but smile.

"Don't worry." He lightly touched her shoulder. Almost of their own accord, his fingers rubbed circles on her bare skin. His blood thickened as desire overtook him.

Vivian stared at him, vulnerable for once. All her defenses were down.

"I should go." He removed his hand reluctantly.

"No." She reached out and grasped his knee. "Please stay."

Javier lowered his gaze to her soft hand on his knee and then raised it to meet her blue eyes. So willing. Without thought, he leaned forward and rested his forehead against hers, looking down. Her nipples tightened against the lace of the nightgown, the thin straps begging to slide off her shoulders, almost disappearing among her hair.

"I believe you, Javier," she whispered. "I believe you." She raised her voice. "I know in my heart it wasn't you."

She believed him. For some reason, the knowledge brought a pleasure that wasn't only sexual.

"Is there another man in your life, Vivian? I need to know," he said, with deliberate restraint, remembering the man she'd called from the restaurant. Could he be a friend, a former lover? Could he be…

"No," she said simply.

Unlike what had happened with Molly, this didn't feel like a mistake. And hell, if it turned out to be one, Vivian would be worth it.

She parted her lips for a kiss. Instead, he eased her down onto the mattress. Unwilling to take her eyes off him, Vivian sighed. She had thought long and hard about this decision. Actually, thinking had been her ally and her captor during the past few days.

During the past six months.

But now, for once she didn't want to think. After getting to know him, after the intense moments they'd shared, she knew she'd been wrong about Javier. Someone else had been responsible for Molly's death. And she would find out whom. Tomorrow.

Not tonight. Tonight, she would declare a truce.

Their bodies molded so perfectly together, Vivian gave a little cry of pleasure. It was unreasonable, she knew, but she wanted Javier inside her as soon as possible. She needed him, and such physical need both disturbed and empowered her.

No waiting.

Javier nibbled her chin, his teeth grazing over her flesh. He kissed her neck, his body brushing unashamedly against hers. He kissed her cheeks, her forehead, and the tip of her nose. When his hot tongue licked her lips, she bucked against him with a moan and opened her mouth wide, desperate for his kiss.

As Vivian opened her legs to accommodate him, her hand searched for his shaft. If he didn't want to thrust into her yet, she would take matters in her own hands. Literally.

"Not yet." He seized her wrist with a grin, then licked her earlobe. His tongue swirled inside the hollow of her ear. She ran both hands through his hair, pulling his head closer.

He carefully removed her nightgown, and she stretched her arms above her head to help. Her underwear slid down her body, leaving a trail of goose bumps. In the past, she'd felt completely exposed when naked with a man. With Javier, a wave of liberation flooded through her when he sucked in his breath.

He stretched her arms apart and pinned her down with gentle firmness, then turned his attention to her breasts.

"*Tan bella.*" Javier licked her hardened nipple, his teeth brushing the tip. She arched her body toward him. The stroke of his tongue drove her into an oversensitive state she couldn't bear.

"I don't know if I get more turned on when you speak Spanish or French," she said. His cool sophistication came through when he spoke French, but in his mother tongue he had a sexy, savage edge that came naturally to him.

His mouth moved to her other breast, his tongue stroking it. Sucking it. Lightly biting.

"*Trop jolie.*"

She closed her eyes. "It's a tie."

"*Schoen,*" he whispered. "German."

"You're showing off." Vivian moaned when he trailed kisses down her rib cage, her skin trembling wherever his tongue licked.

"Enough talking." His husky voice was full of anticipation.

As he moved his body down the bed, she bit her lower lip. His fingers slid between her legs.

She disobeyed his request for silence when he parted her legs. "Javier." He raised his head, his pupils dilated. Seeing him so aroused, his eyes blazing only for her, enhanced her yearning for him.

Vivian shuddered involuntarily when he parted her slick folds with his finger, then stretched her moist walls. As his fingers began to tease her, his tongue licked her thighs. Each time, it branded her skin, moving closer and closer to her most sensitive spot.

She jerked her head back when he licked her inside. He continued stroking her, sucking her, tasting her, and Vivian moaned louder. She lost all sense of herself, all sense of time, and gave herself over to the pleasure, until waves of sensation ripped through her.

When he rose again, slick sweat covering his broad shoulders, she sighed. He stood and left the room.

Vivian raised her head, her heart hammering harder than it had just a few seconds ago. He couldn't simply leave her without a word. Right?

Then, before she could become a victim of her overanalytical mind, he returned with a smirk on his lips and a couple of foil squares in his hand. Relief filled her.

"You came back," she whispered. Her voice carried a layer of emotion she didn't want to label. He frowned for a moment, maybe thinking about what she'd said.

"I had no choice, *mi querida*." His voice was hoarse, his expression tender.

He didn't need to elaborate—not this time. She pulled him closer and kissed him. To hell with the waiting. Her body responded to his with even more urgency than before. The oversensitized place between her legs throbbed with a desire so strong, she doubted either of them would have any power over it.

He groaned when she nibbled on his sexy lips, and when his large hands separated her damp thighs, she threw her head back. His fingers made invisible circles around her thighs as he continued to kiss her mouth, her neck, her shoulders. Each time he came close to touching her more intimately, he would intensify the kiss. When his finger finally made it all the way inside her, she begged, "Now."

He lay down beside her, covered his length, and positioned his body on top of hers.

She opened her legs for him, and he thrust deep, fully awakening her every sense. She wrapped her legs around his hips, panting when they started the sweet dance, his cock moving in and out of her, each time going harder, going deeper.

His mouth finally lowered to hers, his fingers threading in her hair and the deep pressure of his hand massaging her scalp. With visceral need, Vivian clenched her legs around him, tightening her muscles, and embraced him as close as she could. Tides of pleasure rode her body. When her release came, she screamed his name, and he watched her, rapt. As she quivered beneath him, he jerked his head back, and with a final, deep thrust, murmured in Spanish as his body shook above hers.

Chapter Seven

It may have been a few minutes, or maybe several hours. Time seemed to stand still, and the only sound Vivian could hear after their breathing returned to normal was the soothing rhythm of Javier's heartbeat against her ear. They lay together, entangled.

"Javier," she murmured, playing with his chest hair.

"Vivian Foster." He ruffled her hair with his fingers. "I finally have you where I've wanted you all along."

At another time, she would have reacted to his arrogance, but she heard the lightness of his tone, and she was too blissful to protest. Vivian propped herself up on an elbow and raised her head to look at him. "Finally? It wasn't such a long wait."

What a handsome man… His eyes glowed with an emotion she couldn't describe. It quickened her pulse. Shouldn't this be awkward, as it had been with her past boyfriends?

For some reason, it wasn't. All she could do was drink in his male beauty, the awareness he raised in her, and smile at him. If all she had was this one night, she would make the best of it.

"That's where you are wrong, *querida*. It was a long, tormenting wait." His voice was silky. He outlined her jaw with his finger. "But worth every nanosecond."

He was talking about what they had just shared in bed, about the sex. A faint light glowed in the depths of his mercurial eyes, the hidden promise making her blood pound thick and hot. "Did the bodyguard see you when you ran to your bedroom to get the condoms?"

She imagined the look on the man's face when a sweat-slicked Javier rushed from one room into the other.

He chuckled. "You aren't good at pillow talk, are you?"

She couldn't help but laugh. "Add it to my list of flaws."

His fingers rubbed her cheek softly, and she closed her eyes like a pampered cat, soaking in the tenderness. "The list isn't very long," he said huskily.

Vivian opened her eyes to him. Surely he meant the comment sexually. So why did her heart pump with renewed excitement? Though the idea was crazy, could there be something more?

No. She could feel him growing hard against the softness of her thigh. This was only sexual. *I can't fool myself.*

She flipped over him, straddling him before he could react. "You would be surprised."

She leaned down to kiss him. A cold tremor coursed through her. It was because he'd pinched her breast—it had nothing to do with the warning light flickering inside her.

Nothing.

Vivian rolled over, and when no warm body stopped her from nearly falling out of bed, she opened her eyes. His manly scent lingered on the rumpled sheets, but Javier wasn't in them. The only relief to the room's darkness was a thread of light trespassing under the door.

She turned on the lamp, got out of bed, and went to the closet, where she slipped on the lacy white robe that matched the nightgown she no longer wore.

Had he returned to his own bedroom? Had he left her there without so much as a note? Perhaps the bodyguard had turned a light on, though it would be out of character. They were so unobtrusive.

With her heart unsteady, she opened her bedroom door and stepped into the brighter hallway light. She heard the buzzing sound of a television nearby. There was no sign of any bodyguard.

A hearty laugh drifted from the living area—a sound she couldn't associate with the stuffy bodyguard. She moved closer and stepped around the sofa to see Javier in front of the television with a bucket of popcorn on his lap. God, did room service work this late?

She glanced at the black-and-white screen. "The Three Stooges?"

He turned to look at her and smiled carelessly, his eyes gleaming. "I couldn't sleep."

She folded her arms. "Because I was next to you?"

"Yes, because you were next to me, and I didn't have any more condoms."

His honesty caught her off-guard, but she could hardly resist the compliment. She sat beside him, and he threw an arm around her and drew her close. "I guess I can keep it a secret that the big bad CEO likes the Three Stooges," she said.

"You will be generously rewarded." He threw a piece of popcorn at her. It fell down her neckline. She scooped it up and ate it.

Javier smiled and offered her some more. As she bit into the buttery treat, her attention alternated between watching the black-and-white short film and looking at Javier. How could she not steal sideways glances at his relaxed, completely-at-ease profile? She'd never seen him like this before.

One of the Stooges hit another with a mallet—she never could keep them straight—and they laughed. The genuine sound of his pleasure caused a tingle of excitement to make waves inside her. It was all so…domestic. Different from the glamorous dinners, the expensive clothes, the stroll along the Seine. This made her feel as if she and Javier were just like anybody else. Or that they could be, if everything were different.

She forced herself to focus on the present. Right now, it felt great being like everyone else.

He raised the remote and lowered the volume after the ending credits. "When I was a kid, I wanted to be the fourth one."

She almost choked on the popcorn she was eating. "Really? You? A Stooge?"

He chuckled. "I'm not saying I'd have been good at it."

"I don't know which surprises me most—your humility or your comedic ambitions."

He laughed. "Didn't you have any embarrassing childhood ambitions?"

She looked up at the ceiling, trying to recall silly aspirations. "Not that I remember, though I have a pathetic nickname for you. When I started to overtake my classmates in height, they began to call me Vivizon."

He winked. "Vivizon? That's kind of sexy." And just like that, he had turned her shame into something deliciously different.

"I doubt those dreadful boys thought so."

He pulled her closer to him. "You know little about boys, *mi querida*… I'm confident they were just vying for your attention." He displayed a smile capable of melting blocks of ice. "I would have been. If I had known you when I was a little boy, maybe I would have had better things in mind than dreaming of being a Stooge."

Javier planted a kiss on the top of her head. She stared at the rug, processing what he had just told her, but he didn't allow her to continue for long. As if he were reading her mind, he lifted her chin and dipped his head down to hers.

The kiss that followed was warm, sweet, and arousing in a completely different way than the ones they'd shared before. The gentleness of his tongue as it stroked hers sent fast, liquefying heat to her belly.

She panted when his lips left hers. "You said there were no more condoms."

He grinned. "There weren't. I sent the bodyguard on a mission."

"And are you sure you don't want to watch more?" She glanced at the television, where another Stooges show had come on. "I'd hate to take you away from your secret indulgence."

"Like I said...you are worth skipping the Stooges for," he said lightly, and he pushed her down onto the couch with another deep kiss.

Vivian folded the note Javier had placed on the pillow before he'd left and slipped it into her purse. *Returned to my room to take a shower. I hope you aren't too sore. Come get me. Javier.*

Get him? She didn't stand a chance. She had stalled getting out of bed, enjoying the sweet aftermath from the previous night. Memories of their lovemaking flashed in her mind. Truly get him? Maybe not—but she certainly wouldn't forget him.

Eventually, she'd managed to drag herself out of bed to shower. Now as she curled her fingers into her palm to knock on his door, her breath caught in her chest. This was no typical "morning after" situation. Her cheerful, flower-patterned dress paired with green wedge-heeled sandals had an easygoing flair Vivian wished she could claim as her own.

Javier pulled the door open immediately. She cleared her throat, staring at his powerful frame clothed in a dark gray designer suit.

The way he looked at her made her feel like a rare and exotic artifact. She couldn't help but smile.

"Come in," he said.

She felt the blood rush to her face.

She followed him into his room, which was much larger than hers. The king-size bed was adorned with a thick coverlet and a pile of soft pillows. His desk held an empty coffee mug, his laptop, and the pages of a newspaper spread across the polished wood. She swallowed the insecurities knotting her throat.

"Javier, we need to talk." Her fingers fidgeted, and she folded her arms and tucked them away. "Especially after what happened last night."

"I'll go first." He closed the gap between them. He took her hand and kissed the back of it.

She tried to move it away from his hold, but no luck. "Stay with me," he said. "I have an important meeting today, but after that I'll be free for a few days. Instead of flying back tonight, stay with me."

Vivian hesitated, the surprise of his proposal stopping her in her tracks.

For a moment, a complete stillness spread through the room, and she felt as though they were in a lifeless painting like the ones she had seen at the Louvre the previous day.

Until he spoke again.

"I want you in my life, Vivian." His voice was determined, and the way he entwined his fingers with hers got her pulse pounding.

In his life? That had never been part of the plan.

He had to be joking. A cruel joke. Though the warmth in his eyes almost made her consider it—which was madness.

She had to tell him. She had to tell him the missing bit about her revenge plan. And if he still wanted her in his life after that, well, they'd revisit the idea…

Though I doubt he will.

Vivian grasped his hand tightly before pulling her fingers from his. "Javier, we need to talk."

"We will, *mi querida*. We'll talk…among other things." He embraced her again, kissing her briefly before she could deny him. His phone rang, but he ignored it.

"This is hard," she muttered, pressing her lips together.

"Are you softening up, Vivian Foster?" He shot her a smile so adorable, her stomach clenched.

His phone stopped ringing. A short beep announced a text message.

Javier sighed. "Just a moment, it might be important." He walked to his bedside table, scooped the phone up in one quick move, and read the message.

"This has to be a mistake." He shook his head and quickly made a phone call.

Javier paced in circles, mumbling in Spanish, before he turned his back to her and faced outside as he listened to a message. She followed his gaze. The sky was heavily overcast, the Eiffel Tower drab and gray. She waited for the storm to break.

Javier finished his call.

"What is it?" Vivian asked, the blood pounding in her head.

"I was supposed to sign a big contract today. My lawyer just notified me that it's been delayed."

Vivian bit her lip. "Javier…" Emotion clogged her throat.

His phone rang again. The thudding of her heart filled the room.

This time, he glanced at it and stiffened, the tension in his shoulders pulling his jacket tight across his upper back. He didn't answer the phone. Instead he put it in his pocket.

She could tell he had just realized it.

"You," he accused her.

"I'm sorry."

For a long time, he remained motionless.

Then he turned to her, and she stared into his angry face.

"Why are you sorry?" he asked. His eyes were hard and cold, his voice controlled.

Vivian reached up with shaking fingers and wiped the light sheen of sweat from her forehead. She massaged her temple for a few seconds, needing to ease the headache that had come upon her. "I told Edouard Broussard my suspicions about Molly. He's probably delaying the merger to investigate."

"You stabbed me in the back." She could almost taste the bitterness in his voice.

Vivian looked deep into his eyes. "It was before I believed you were innocent."

His phone started to beep again. She imagined he had an army of lawyers, team merger staff, and probably even the press trying to reach him.

Javier finally took the phone from his pocket, his fingers scrolling through the new messages until he singled one out and read it aloud. "*I want to see you both in my office immediately. Edouard.*" After a pause, he said, "I can't believe you told him this fabrication. I could sue you for defamation."

Where was the man who had asked her to stay with him?

Vivian stared out the window as thick droplets of water fell from the sky onto the terrace.

"Someone killed Molly. Not you, but someone else." She

moved to close the French doors so the wind wouldn't blow the rain inside, but she stopped short. Did she really want to feel even more confined with this man who glared at her as if she were lower than dirt?

"When did you tell him?"

"I mentioned it at the fund-raiser party and explained it further yesterday."

"At the dinner party. How convenient." He shot her a glance of pure repugnance. "Why didn't he say anything to me?"

"He told me he'd look into it. Maybe he found something. Maybe that's why he delayed the merger signing."

"I thought you weren't like the others, Vivian. I was mistaken." He looked her up and down. The sheer disappointment in his expression made her temples throb more than when he'd insulted her a few minutes ago. "You are far worse."

"I was about to tell you, before your telephone call," Vivian said. She kept her voice gentle, hoping to avoid an argument.

His sarcastic laughter washed over her. "You expect me to believe that?"

"I didn't tell you when you asked me in the restaurant because I didn't trust you, but then I started to have doubts. I started to believe you even before I could admit it to myself. I wouldn't have given myself if I didn't believe you."

"Given yourself? Just because we had sex? That's rich," he snarled. "All along, all you've wanted to do was to take."

"That's not true… I haven't taken anything yet." Her voice gained strength at the end, though she hadn't meant to challenge him.

"Well, get ready, *princesa*. I will sort this out and still get what I want." Javier snorted, staring at her. His silent message that she was playing with fire and out of her depth had come too late. "Although I'll admit, you've scored your points. If your goal was to humiliate me, I'm sure what I've just said to you was the highlight of your weekend."

She shook her head. "No, that was never part of the plan."

Never.

I want you in my life, Vivian. His words to her echoed in her mind.

Just minutes ago, he had wanted her to stay with him. The intimacy in his tone, the earnestness had suggested he wanted more than a few days after the celebration of a big contract.

Don't fool yourself.

If he'd wanted her in his life for the longer term—or until he tired of her in the bedroom—would he really have changed so drastically from hot to cold without considering her motives?

It didn't matter. It *shouldn't* matter anymore what he had implied.

But a small, quiet part of her insisted that it did.

"Let's go," he said, grabbing his briefcase. "Let's sort this out."

Subject closed.

Continuous phone calls and text messages held his attention and gave her momentary relief during the drive from the hotel. He switched from English to French and back, assuring his lawyers and merger team that he was about to take care of the merger and never once mentioning her or any sort of plan.

"It's a minor setback," he said. "I'm dealing with it right now." He shot her a warning stare that told her she'd better not try to cross him again. She looked out the window as the limousine entered La Défense, the financial district just outside Paris.

"What else did you tell Edouard?" he asked after he'd hung up.

"I shared my concern with him."

"For him to delay the deal, you must have shared a lot more." Disbelief and disapproval flickered in his eyes. "There has to be another reason you would do this. Not just your friendship with Molly." He narrowed his eyes, as if by focusing his vision on her face he could force the truth out of her. "You cannot be so loyal to her, yet so treacherous to me."

"To a cynical man like you, maybe friendship isn't enough." She clenched her hands. "It wasn't easy. Whatever you think of me, I don't like lying and deceiving."

"Vivian, I don't care what you like. As long as you know this: you aren't going to steal this from me. I've worked too hard and too long to let it slip through my fingers."

"Is that a threat?"

"That was a statement. I can sue you for industrial espionage and make sure you don't find a job anywhere in London."

"And you still don't see why I couldn't trust you at first?" She managed a short laugh to conceal her uneasiness.

This man can ruin my life. No, wait—he will *ruin it.*

"Given what you have done, threatening you with fair legal action does not make me untrustworthy," he said coldly.

She was walking on a tightrope. She only hoped she could make it to the other end without falling. There would be no safety net below her.

The limousine pulled to a stop before the imposing Broussard corporate office building.

They emerged from the car, and a bodyguard appeared behind them. He must have arrived in a different vehicle. "Is this really necessary?" Vivian asked as all three of them walked inside the building.

"I don't want you to run away," he said, guiding her into the elevator.

"I won't run away." She lifted her chin. "I will cooperate

to the very end to make sure justice is done."

Maybe now that Edouard had an interest in Molly's death, she could get access to the resources she needed to find the killer.

"You lied to me all the time, seduced me as part of your scheme, and suddenly you are Lady Justice," Javier said as they reached the top floor.

"I did not *try* to seduce you." Vivian raised her eyes to meet his. "It was rather the other way around."

"You won't have to worry about that anymore." His eyes pinned her down, the mistrust sending a tremor through her body. "From now on, I will not lay one finger on you, Vivian Foster." With a curse under his breath, he leaned closer. "I can't wait to have you out of my sight."

Chapter Eight

They held each other's gaze for a long moment before Vivian let her eyes drift away. The tightrope came to mind again, and she closed her fists. She felt her sweaty toes curling around the rope, her body shifting weight to avoid a fall.

Vivian shrugged the awareness off. "I can't wait either."

He continued to stare without speaking, the disdain in his black eyes more disturbing than his size as he towered over her. When she had first met him in her office, she'd thought him ruthless and driven. But as he broke their stare and strode into Edouard's office, Javier became some kind of CEO warrior, unwilling to let go of his merger no matter what. Vivian followed, matching his pace.

They passed by Edouard's secretary, who asked them to wait in his office since Edouard was busy in the conference room. Shaking his head angrily, Javier proceeded to the conference room.

"The door is closed," Vivian said when they got there.

She could hear voices through the closed door. Javier must have heard them, too, because he frowned as he listened.

One of the speakers was Edouard Broussard, she was sure, but the other voice—although it had a familiar timbre—wasn't loud enough for her to recognize.

"Wait here. Don't move." Javier's voice sounded as though it was made of steel. He opened one of the doors without knocking and walked into the conference room.

She glanced at the bodyguard, then exhaled and tried to peek through the open door. When she moved closer, the bodyguard blocked her view with a swift move to the left.

"I'll go in eventually, anyway." Vivian cleared her throat, turning to the glass wall that displayed the Eiffel Tower in the background and the street below. What she wouldn't give to be just someone strolling down the streets of Paris, carefree.

But this is what I wanted...to serve as an instrument in Molly's revenge.

She ran her fingers through her hair. The minutes dragged.

Vivian stared at the door. Although she couldn't understand what was being said, there were at least three distinct voices, then silence.

Finally, a tall man emerged from the conference room. *Roger.*

"I will wait for your decision, Edouard," he said.

Vivian pointed at him. "You." How had Roger gathered that Edouard was going to delay the merger signing so quickly? She hadn't talked to him after dinner last night—hadn't given him any thought at all since she'd last spoken to him.

"Vivian Foster." He bowed his head and offered her a cynical smile.

"How did you—" Vivian started.

"How did he what?" Javier emerged from the conference room and cut her off angrily. She opened her mouth, then paused.

"Nicely done, Vivian." The man winked at her, then

turned to Javier and gave him a look she couldn't read.

"How do you know him?" Javier asked under his breath.

"She was a great help to me," Roger answered for her, with a smirk.

Vivian felt her brows furrowing as she tried to understand what had just happened. Why would Roger make it clear to Javier that they knew each other? And what was he doing walking out of Edouard's conference room, looking as though he'd won some kind of prize?

Roger didn't stick around to provide any answers. He turned his back and walked out of the room, and Javier stared down at her, a puzzled look on his face.

"It is him, isn't it? The man you called from that restaurant is Easton Finn," he said.

Easton Finn?

"If that's his real name, then yes. He told me to call him Roger," she said at last, still stunned that Roger had purposely exposed her to Javier and then disappeared.

Judging by Javier's hateful expression, he knew all there was to know about Easton Finn, and none of it was good.

His jaw clenched. "That man wants to destroy all I have worked for, and you've helped him."

"He wanted you out of the merger, yes. That's all I know."

"Now I understand why Easton was here. You warned him the deal would be delayed, and he was eager to put his claws in my merger."

Vivian crossed her arms, taking a deep breath and a step back. Before she could say anything, Edouard appeared, frowning. "I need to talk to both of you." His tone was much firmer than it had been on the other occasions he had spoken to her. "Now."

Vivian followed the two men into the conference room in silence. It was a spacious room, with a big oval-shaped oak table and several beige leather chairs around it.

She shook with anxiety. What if the Frenchman was about to tell her that he not only didn't believe her, but he would take some sort of legal action against her for delaying a billion-pound merger? Could he even do such a thing?

Javier could. He could talk to his solicitors, and they would use her snooping in his office, trying to mess up his deal, as evidence to get in her in serious trouble with the law.

"Please sit down." They sat. "Vivian, you have asked me to look into Molly Richardson's death. Javier, I have a couple of questions for you. Did you sleep with Molly?"

Javier gave an impatient sigh, obviously not pleased to have his private life on display. "Once."

Edouard shook his head. "And then you fired her."

"No. I made a mistake. Once, after a happy hour, I...got involved with her. It was an error in judgment. The next day, I apologized and explained it would be best if we forgot what had happened. Although she agreed, I could tell she was upset. A couple of weeks later, someone from the merger team came to see me and told me they suspected Molly was taking confidential information home. We looked into it, and once we knew for sure she intended to sell company information to someone, I fired her."

Edouard shifted his head in her direction. "Does this seem right to you?"

Did it? Vivian blinked, still taken aback by Javier's version of the facts. "I spoke to Molly. She told me they had an affair. And also that she sought out his opponent, Roger—I mean Easton Finn—after Javier fired her because he didn't want to sleep with her anymore."

"This is absurd. I would never do something like that." He turned to Vivian, glaring at her for the first time during the conversation. "Did I take advantage of you during the time we were together?"

Edouard scratched his chin. "You two got involved." It

sounded more like an accusation than a question.

Vivian felt the heat spreading across her face. She glanced at Javier. "You didn't take advantage of me. I don't have any complaints."

"Firing Molly was the nice thing to do. I could have sued her, but I let her go," Javier told Edouard.

"I know that Javier didn't kill her," Vivian told Edouard. "He's convinced me of that. But I'm sure someone did."

"How about the investigator? Do we have anything on him?"

"I doubt it." Javier reached for his phone and retrieved the contact information on the touch screen. "But I can give you his contact information." He picked up a notepad, scribbled some words on it, and handed it to Edouard. "His name is Matt Smith. He has been a loyal employee whenever we needed anyone investigated."

"Could Finn have hired the two men to stalk her?" Vivian asked.

"Why would he scare Molly when she was on his side?" Javier asked.

It made sense. Molly had been nothing but helpful to Easton Finn, and at no cost to him.

"I don't know what happened," Javier said. "Molly was unstable. Who knows what kind of people she got mixed up with? All I know is I had nothing to do with her death."

"Well," Edouard intervened, his expression focused and alert. "I need to make a decision."

"What decision? She just admitted she was wrong."

"Javier, I can't sign a merger with you if there is any possibility you'd be linked to the death or suicide of this girl. It would be wrong on a personal level, and professionally I can't compromise my business interests or my foundation. I need more information. My investigator tells me Molly's only living relative is her mother, who lives in Switzerland. Perhaps she can help us to understand what happened, if there's a chance Molly suffered from any illness Vivian didn't know about."

"That's a terrible idea," Vivian said, remembering how aloof Molly's mother had been after the funeral. She'd flown out of England as quickly as she could, barely saying a word to Vivian.

"I say, question her mother," Javier said.

Edouard snapped his fingers. "This is a delicate matter. It should be dealt with personally, but I don't want to get involved more than necessary. You must handle it." He looked at Javier. "Fly to Switzerland and talk to Molly's mother. See if she knows anything that will help us assess what happened. Get it recorded and come back to me tomorrow with it."

"I will."

"How can you be sure the woman he'll talk to is Molly's mom? It could be anyone. He doesn't even need to leave the country," Vivian said.

"You'll go with him," Edouard said with calm confidence. "You both have strong reasons to discover what happened, and I trust you more than an investigator. Javier, if you didn't torment this woman to death, you will get your deal signed as soon as you come back. But if I have doubts about how you handled yourself, I will have to cancel our merger agreement, and perhaps even consider Easton Finn's proposal, since he's so interested." Edouard stood up.

"How are we supposed to find her mother?" Vivian asked.

"This is the address my investigator located." Edouard handed a piece of paper to Javier. "Now I have to deal with the press speculating about the merger. Off you go. I expect to hear from you tomorrow." Edouard clicked one of the many flashing lights on the phone on the conference table.

No wonder he had a coveted empire. When it was time to do business, the man worked swiftly.

"How long will the flight be?" Vivian asked when they boarded Javier's private jet.

"Not long." He sat down across from her. He could have picked any other seat. If he wanted to, he could have chosen not to even look at her.

But not looking at her was impossible.

He had to look at her to remind himself of how stupid he had been to nearly fall for the woman whose sole purpose was to ruin his life. Vivian Foster, who had lied to him and used him to please another man.

Just like my mother.

"What was Easton doing at Edouard's office when we got there?"

"He was trying to persuade Edouard to consider his offer for the merger instead of mine. When did you speak with him last?"

Vivian sighed. "Yesterday."

"How?"

"I bought a prepaid mobile at the souvenir shop. You may as well know it. I'm done with lying."

"I paid for a mobile for you to call Easton." He couldn't keep the bitterness from his voice.

"I'm sorry, but it was the only way. I didn't have my wallet or any money."

Out of all his rivals, Vivian had teamed up with Easton.

Not only that, he had touched her. He had *had* her.

Javier clenched his fists so tightly, his nails broke the skin.

Easton Finn…his lifelong opponent and enemy, who was supposed to have been dormant, had awakened again. They hadn't crossed paths in more than five years, when Easton outbid him at the last minute for a piece of prime real estate in New York. Javier hadn't given Easton's business antics much thought lately, since his investigator had found no signs of sabotage. Even when Molly had been caught taking confidential information home, there had been no sign of Finn's involvement. They had investigated with no success, assuming that perhaps she'd intended to sell to the highest bidder. And hell, he knew he had quite a few opponents out there who'd love to sink their claws into the merger.

The old man was slick.

How could I let Vivian occupy a place in my mind that should have focused only on the merger?

The woman he thought worth his time and his bed, the strong woman with a vulnerability that had inspired him to dig deep and expose his own hidden weaknesses, his past... That woman had been a lie.

"No bodyguard?" Vivian asked.

"It's just you and me," he said. Javier wanted as few people around them as possible. Although he trusted his bodyguard, he didn't want anyone to tell Easton of their whereabouts. "I intend to find this woman. If you have any tricks up your sleeve, forget them."

"Why would I have tricks up my sleeve?"

He didn't know. He worried when he couldn't read her thoughts. The blend of her lavender and orchid scent surrounded him, her perfume lingering in the aircraft.

"To buy Easton time. To get me out of the race."

"Javier, I know now that you didn't kill Molly. I'll have nothing further to do with Easton. But there are some unanswered questions, and although I doubt her mother will be a big help, I'm on board." A pang of sadness laced her voice.

Just an act.

"Do you have any idea what you have done? Because of your unfounded suspicions, a major business deal has been delayed. I have lots of people who depend on me whose jobs are on the line."

"I didn't know you were so altruistic." Her voice carried sarcasm, or perhaps surprise. He couldn't really tell any longer.

"I'm fair. What did Easton promise you, money?" The anger rose up—anger with himself for his inability to drop the subject. It was the idea of Easton being involved. Easton and Vivian.

"Money doesn't interest me."

"Why not? Do you have plenty of it?" He wondered if Easton had bought her jewelry or other expensive gifts. His chest tightened as he imagined Vivian in bed with the old bastard.

He would not allow himself to care who she'd slept with.

"I don't have plenty of it." She gave him a dismissive shrug, as if she didn't care or money didn't matter to her.

What a joke.

The flight attendant entered the cabin, smiling as she handed him a glass of scotch and gave Vivian a glass of orange juice. He usually didn't drink during the day, but he needed something to settle the turmoil of his feelings.

He watched her as she drank her juice, torn between wanting her to disappear from his life and wanting her so badly it was a physical ache.

Wanting her after everything she'd done—it was a new low. But the idea of pulling her to him, ripping her clothes off, and taking her in the most primitive fashion wouldn't leave his mind. Whatever sexual spell she'd spun around him was still pulsing, just like a part of him he wished wasn't.

Javier pulled the tray closer over his erection. His own body had betrayed him.

"How can you be loyal to a lover who didn't care if you slept with another man?" He had to know.

"Who, Easton?" She flipped the pages of a business magazine she had picked out from the built-in shelf next to the window. "He wasn't my lover."

"I don't believe you."

"I told you there was no man in my life, remember?"

"Well, he is nothing but a dirtbag. Not a man. But still, that's just terminology."

"I didn't lie to you about him." She closed the magazine and glanced around before her blue eyes found his.

"What else didn't you lie about?"

It didn't matter anymore, but he wanted to know it all. "Your parents? Your upbringing?" His voice rose as he spoke.

"I didn't lie about my parents or my life in general. I lied about why I was in your office, and it grew from there. But I did that because I had a purpose."

Javier managed a terse laugh. "How did you meet Easton?"

"Molly approached him because she knew he was also very interested in the merger. After her funeral, he came to me—the only time we've met in person—and proposed that I continue what she'd started."

"You've met him in person only once?" Javier snorted. "I don't buy it."

"I'm not going to keep apologizing to you for lying," Vivian said. "You obviously hate me and don't believe anything I say…and I don't care what you think of me at this point." She gave him a long, assessing look before opening the magazine again.

"Now that I can believe," he said drily, raising his glass of scotch in a toast.

The jet landed smoothly forty minutes later, and they swiftly passed through immigration. The top-of-the-line German sedan Javier had requested from the rental desk as they traveled was waiting.

"No limo this time?" Vivian asked.

"The fewer people are involved in this, the better."

Why is she so worried about being alone with me?

Javier shook his head. She wasn't. Maybe she had counted on having either the bodyguard or a chauffeur around to distract him, or hoped she might persuade them to help her send Easton a message.

Javier held the steering wheel tightly as they turned onto the main road to the city.

It was a cool, sunny day, and Lake Zurich was crowded. Children chattered and squealed as they cheekily threw food to the ducks on the lake. A couple of stylishly dressed women walked their tiny dogs around the plaza, and cars fought for parking spaces. The traffic was slow and chaotic, just as he had expected. Downtown, tourists hopped on the city trolley, which made annoying, continuous stops. Blue-collar workers took the train to get into the city. It seemed that everywhere he looked, everyone was rushing to get somewhere.

Infierno. None of it took his mind off the woman sitting next to him. He could not get the dreadful image of Vivian with Easton out of his head. He needed to focus on securing his merger without allowing himself to be distracted by her presence, either in his head or by his side.

"It's daytime. What if she's working?" Vivian asked when he parked on the street in a middle-class neighborhood.

"Then I will find out where she works." Javier got out of the car.

They walked in silence on the narrow sidewalk of an even narrower street, past a couple of restaurants and flower shops, until they reached a faded brown townhouse and Javier confirmed the number above the door.

He buzzed the intercom, but there was no answer. As he sighed in frustration, an elderly woman carrying a bag of groceries approached the narrow iron gate. She opened the door with an access key, and when Javier heard the clicking noise, he opened the door wide for her, smiling politely.

She smiled back and mumbled a thank-you as she walked in. Javier pretended to look for his keys until the lady was out of sight, then caught the door before it fully closed. He looked at Vivian as they entered the building.

"No elevator. Great." She shuddered at the sight of an old stairwell. "What floor does she live on?"

"Fourth." Javier regretted letting her walk ahead of him as they climbed the stairs. They were careful to stay a few steps behind the old lady, who had also taken the stairs. The last thing they needed was unwanted attention.

He looked away from Vivian's perfectly rounded bottom, which swayed with every step.

The narrow stairwell seemed to close in on him, as he wondered what it would be like to take her right here against the wall or on the steps. To rid his body of the poisonous need.

To his relief, they soon reached the fourth floor.

"Maybe she's out," Vivian said after she knocked on the door a few times. "Or working."

He spotted the lady across the hall, still fighting to find the key in her purse while balancing grocery bags. Vivian approached her and stretched her hand out with a warm smile. "Here, I can help," she offered.

The lady handed her the bags, and after retrieving the apartment key in her purse, she opened her arms to get her bags back. "Thank you."

"My pleasure." Vivian carefully handed them back. "By the way, do you know what time the lady from 4C will return? I was a friend of her daughter's."

The old lady smiled. "Laura's on vacation. She left for Zuoz to go hiking. She does that every year in the spring."

"Do you know where she stays in Zuoz?" Javier asked.

The lady wrinkled her forehead in thought. "A cozy little place that has a statue of two birds at the entrance. But I don't know the name."

"Thank you," Vivian said.

"I'll tell her you stopped by."

"That won't be necessary," Javier said. "We'll go and visit her in Zuoz."

Chapter Nine

"We're here," Javier said, and Vivian woke, startled and disoriented. Her last memory before her lids closed had been of the pastel colors of the sunset over peaceful countryside, which, along with the slowed rhythm of the car, had lulled her into a doze.

She followed Javier from the car and smiled at the entrance to a dark-brown lodge with a medium-sized stone statue of two kissing birds in the front garden. If things weren't so strained between them, she would have congratulated him on his acute sense of direction, as he had only glanced at the map once before finding the street filled with bed-and-breakfasts.

At the run-down reception area, Javier spoke in German with the receptionist. Vivian picked up a brochure for visitors and pretended to read while she watched Javier.

She knew Molly hadn't committed suicide. Aside from that truth, all she had were questions. Did Molly have an affair with someone else? Could there be another explanation? Would Edouard get something out of Javier's investigator?

"Vivian," Javier called. "Laura Richardson isn't here."

"She's not?" Vivian blinked out of her trance.

"She's been staying here, but she has gone hiking in the woods for a couple of days."

Vivian looked at the forest through the big window. Darkness blanketed the trees. "She went in there."

Javier nodded. "Yes. And so will we."

"I don't think so." Vivian crossed her arms. "It's getting dark." The prospect of adventuring into the gloomy forest with Javier after such a long day was not at all favorable. She hadn't eaten on the flight. Her anxiety had been stronger than any desire for food. Now she was starving. "If we succeed at anything apart from dying of exhaustion, it will be scaring her to death. We can't turn up in the middle of the night."

"Are you trying to delay this from happening?" Javier stepped closer, his mocking, disbelieving eyes capturing hers.

"I'm starving. And not dressed to wander into the woods." She smoothed her dress with her hands and avoided looking at his dark gray suit, which fit his large body perfectly.

Javier paused for a moment, then turned to speak to the receptionist. He tucked a key ring into his pocket and turned back to her.

"All right. There's a restaurant down the street. We can eat something, then sleep and depart to look for her tomorrow, first thing in the morning."

"Thank you." Vivian smiled with relief, but he didn't smile in return.

They chose to stroll to the restaurant. Javier was silent as they made their way to the Italian bistro.

Vivian took in the tall streetlamps shining down a street filled with cozy bistros, small antique shops, and a crowded plaza, where some people enjoyed the breezy evening and chatted.

During their meal, Javier checked the voice mails and text messages on his phone and completely ignored her. She pondered. Should she eat in silence and pretend not to care? But the day had been long. Her defenses were long since exhausted, and after all, she had told him the truth. She'd unlocked all the secrets of her motives for him. Why shouldn't he do the same?

"Why does this merger matter so much to you?" she asked.

He raised his eyes from the phone to hers, frowning slightly. "I'm not in the mood for small talk."

"It can't be just the money. You're a wealthy man."

He sat up straight, flashing her a look full of contempt. He was not the least bit interested in having this conversation with her.

"I told you what moved me," she pressed. "I want know that the reason you've done all you've done to protect this merger isn't just money."

After all, I've risked everything. I've gone against one of the most powerful men in England, who now hates me and has assured me he will make my life hell.

She didn't even want to think about what that would entail.

"Why?" he asked. "Does everything need a noble reason to justify it?"

Earlier, he'd made a point of warning her that if the merger fell through, people would lose their jobs. She felt enough guilt about that to fill Lake Zurich. But she knew creating or saving jobs hadn't been his motivation. Something else had triggered his relentless pursuit of the Broussard empire.

"No, not everything." She shrugged, her fingers playing with her fork over her half-eaten pasta.

"Even if I did have a reason, why would I share it with you?"

"Sharing real feelings doesn't make you inferior, Javier."

For several minutes, he didn't say anything. While

he finished eating, his eyes fixed on something past her, something that wasn't there, she let herself feel how much she missed him. How she missed the little time she had spent with what she thought of as the real Javier—the man behind the mask, who had problems and traumas and insecurities like anyone else. The man who had made her feel important and cherished when he'd opened the gate to his past, something he obviously didn't do often.

That man is gone.

Javier pushed to his feet. "Time to go." He took out a few bills and placed them on the table.

As they headed back, Vivian dwelled on her memories of their short days in Paris. The way her skin had responded to his touch. How he'd helped her to overcome old insecurities.

She was so absorbed in her thoughts, she inhaled in shock when Javier's arm snaked around her waist and he pulled her off the street into a dark alley.

His hand covered her mouth. "Shh."

He was dangerously close, and she looked past him. She could make out nothing but the Dumpster nearby and a couple of sleeping alley cats. A ray of light from the streetlamp showed the worry etched on his face.

When he removed his hand from her mouth, she whispered, "What are you doing?"

Javier looked over his shoulder, and so did she. A man was walking down the street they had been on. Javier must have known who he was and why he was important, but Vivian had no idea what was happening.

Not that she minded being close to him once again. Her body responded to his with an unsettling tingle in the pit of her stomach.

As if he'd sensed it, he stepped back.

"Javier, what is it?"

"I'm making sure we aren't being followed," he said.

"That man was at the restaurant, and he left right after we did."

Vivian shook her head. "Why would we be followed?"

"Maybe Easton doesn't want me to find Molly's mother. Maybe he's found her already and paid her off."

He kept looking at the man, and to Vivian's relief, a woman and a laughing child joined him, and they walked to a sedan parked off the narrow street. Javier sighed.

"Javier, you need some rest. I'm not an idiot. I gather that Easton isn't a good man, but — "

"*Now* you agree with me," he said drily. They left the alley and began walking back to the bed-and-breakfast.

Vivian glared back at him, and even in the dim light, she could see his dark eyes blaze with resentment. "He could have pretended not to know me when he saw me earlier in Edouard's office," she pointed out. "But he made sure he called me by name. He wanted to expose me to you. He wanted for you to know that I was part of his plan."

He nodded.

Well, at least they agreed about one thing.

They walked in silence for a few minutes. "If he hadn't exposed you, would you have told me?" he asked.

"Would you believe me if I said yes?"

"No."

"Then he achieved what he wanted to."

"You've done that yourself, Vivian."

She stopped in front of him and looked up into his face. "Javier." He wouldn't meet her eyes. "You said Molly was a one-night stand for you. She led me to believe you two had an affair. Is there a possibility she fell for you and you didn't acknowledge it?"

"I'd had a few drinks, but I didn't behave irresponsibly. When we slept together, I told her I didn't have any more to give. I didn't deceive her."

He didn't have any more to give Molly, or anyone? The question burned at the tip of her tongue. But judging by the seriousness in his expression and the way he picked up his pace, Javier was done with personal conversation.

She couldn't worry about losing him. She'd never had him to lose, not really. All she had was a crazy attraction that had nothing to do with reason, and a suffocating sense of missed opportunity that could never turn into anything more. Sadly for her, she didn't even have an opportunity at the moment to deal with these emotions.

By the time they reached the front door of the cabin, Vivian craved solitude. All she wanted was to close the door of a room, undress, and take a long, hot shower. And cry. She could already feel her cheeks hardening, the warm pressure building beneath her forehead. All the tears she'd held back during the course of the day begged for release. "What time do we need to leave tomorrow?"

"Early. I will wake you if you are still sleeping."

"Okay. May I have my room key?" She stretched out her hand.

Javier took a key from his pocket. "Our room. We are sharing it."

"I don't think that's a good idea." Vivian didn't even try to hide her nervousness. It was too late for that.

"Neither do I." He opened the door wide and signaled with his hands for her to go inside. "But I don't trust you, so I have no option."

The small room was quite different from the luxurious suite they'd shared in Paris. The furniture had seen better days. Her gaze moved from the narrow entrance to the wooden chest with a round mirror, to…*one* queen-size bed adorned with a light-green coverlet.

She looked for another bed, but all she could see was a recliner in one corner, a bedside table with an old-fashioned alarm clock and a lamp, and the bathroom door.

She cleared her throat. "This isn't going to work."

"I'll sleep on the chair."

She couldn't *not* notice his slightly husky tone when he pointed to the recliner.

"You won't fit in it." The thought of his large body cramped on the recliner was absurd.

More absurd was the fantasy of her naked body straddling his on that recliner, his strong hands on each side of her waist while she threw her head back with a moan of pure pleasure. He would lick her neck, pinch her hardened nipples, and kiss her.

Vivian blinked the insane image away and cleared her throat again.

"I'll manage," he said casually. "Do you want to use the bathroom first? I want to go to sleep." Though he was a billionaire used to the best things in life, his practical sense impressed her. He didn't make a big deal about the drab room. Even she felt like complaining…but not a word from him. He was willing to fold his large body up in an old, cramped recliner.

Or maybe he just wants to go to sleep?

Vivian disappeared into the small, functional bathroom. She took a shower and hand-washed her bra and panties.

They had left Paris in such a hurry they hadn't packed, and there were no stores open in Zuoz at that time of the evening. She had no option but to wrap herself in a towel. It barely covered her thighs. To her relief, when she passed Javier by, he busied himself with sliding his fingers over the touch screen of his phone. The floor creaked when she was just a couple of steps away from the bed.

He shifted, lifting his eyes from the phone. Slowly, very slowly, his stare rose from her legs up her bare thighs, over her chest, to linger on her face.

Her throat closed as his eyes met hers and their gazes locked together for a few seconds.

Sexy.

Dangerous.

Forbidden.

She couldn't look at him and forget how insanely hot he looked naked. The way his long fingers moved inside her. His hands, relentlessly exploring every part of her body. Making her feel like an empowered, desired, strong woman.

Making her feel.

As if snapping out of a trance, Javier stood up.

He passed by her close enough that she could smell the mixture of his minty aftershave, which still lingered from the morning, and his own male scent. He shut the bathroom door behind him, and soon she heard the water running. Vivian got on the bed, discarded her towel over the side, and quickly pulled the thin sheet and coverlet up over her nakedness.

But not even her nakedness saved her from the scorching sensation blanketing her body. She looked around, hoping to find an air-conditioning unit, even one of those old, loud ones that looked as if they had been fabricated a couple of centuries ago. Even a slow-motion fan would do.

Nothing.

She stared at the ceiling, then around her bed and beyond. No fan.

She had counted on more time to prepare herself for what was to come—ten minutes or longer, although even that would not have been enough. But sooner than she'd wished, she heard the sharp creak of the faucet being turned off. She turned the lamp off just before the door opened, and his steps approached.

She closed her eyes, feigning sleep.

"It's hot in here."

Vivian opened her eyes. The pitch blackness gave her

no view of what he was wearing…or not wearing. The floor creaked under his bare feet, and as he moved closer, her heart beat faster.

"No air-conditioning," Vivian said. "I checked."

"I will open the window." He turned her bedside lamp on.

The light exposed his silk boxers. It also exposed his bare chest, and a throbbing commenced at the juncture of her thighs.

He wasn't paying her any attention. She propped herself up on her elbows, raising her eyes to the large window over the bed. He would have to step onto the bed to reach it.

And that's exactly what he did.

"I can move," she offered, pulling the coverlet up when his foot eased down on the mattress.

"This will only take a second."

One painful second.

Washing her underwear instead of wearing it had not been a good idea. Vivian tightened her legs together, wanting to erase the moisture between them just as she wished she could erase the memories of his shaft thrusting deep and hard into her, his hot tongue teasing the dark corners inside her mouth.

"Much better," Javier said when he popped the window open and a light breeze swept in, the scent of lime trees scenting the fresh air.

He returned to his chair.

She broke the silence. "Good night, Javier."

He didn't respond.

Bright sunlight shone on Vivian's face. She rubbed the back of her hand over her eyes and opened them slowly to take in the morning.

With a yawn, she sat up in the bed, legs crossed and arms wide above her head like a lazy cat stretching. A cough from the other side of the room reminded her she was not alone, and she quickly covered herself with a sheet before glancing across at Javier.

"G-good morning."

He stood, looking away. His hair was wet, and he wore his suit trousers and white shirt again.

"Did I oversleep? How long—"

"I just returned from the reception area. I brought you something to eat." He pointed at the small tray on the top of the dresser. There was a small cup of coffee, a sandwich, and an apple.

"Thank you."

"I have a map. I bought some essentials from the desk attendant." He zipped a sturdy green backpack closed as he spoke. "We still need to stop at a store to get the right clothes to go into the forest."

"Do you have any idea where Laura is?"

"He showed me on the map where she usually goes. It's a popular camping site."

She nodded, reluctant to get out of the bed. Of course she wanted to know if Laura had anything important to say that Vivian already didn't know about Molly. But at the same time, a part of her warned that finding Laura meant she wouldn't see Javier again.

"I'll wait for you outside." He grabbed the backpack and closed the door behind him.

When she dressed and emerged from the room, Javier led her to a small hiking shop. "We don't have much time," he said. The shop had some good and even expensive brands, and the racks were crowded. Javier picked out a pair of jeans and a black T-shirt with the efficiency that was his trademark. Never mind that he had never been to this shop. He worked his way around the rack until he'd selected a few items. "These should work," he announced.

"You're not going to try them on?"

"No need." He went through the racks opposite her and removed a few hangers. He handed her a white-and-green-striped tank top and a pair of faded jeans. "These will do for you."

"What are you, a salesman?" Vivian glanced at the randomly picked pieces, hoping the jeans would fit. She was enjoying this no-frills Javier. One day he sent for extravagant clothes for her in a five-star hotel, the next he was picking the first thing off the rack and not even letting her try it on.

"I'm good at making assumptions. Most of the time." The hint of sarcasm in his voice brought her back to reality.

"Javier, can't we just be cordial with each other? Soon this will all be over." Vivian held the top over her upper body.

"It isn't only about what I want to get, Vivian." Javier's hands tightened around the jeans he carried. "It's also about what I don't wish Easton to have."

"What's that?"

"I don't want to fail." His eyes fixed on the floor for a moment. When he raised his gaze to hers, she saw an uncharacteristic hint of fear in his eyes. "If I can't get the merger and he does…" He trailed off, as if the prospect were too unbearable for him to speak it out loud.

Vivian's breath caught. She looked around them, wishing they were alone. The store clerk had her eyes glued to the small television on the counter. There were a couple of other customers trying on hiking shoes as they spoke in German.

She stepped closer to Javier. "Why does it matter so much? If he gets it?"

She had asked him this before, and her chances of getting an answer now were no better. As Vivian watched, the lines of Javier's face tightened, and his eyes seemed to stare past her for a moment before he turned back to her and gave her his fiercest glare.

"Because that man ruined my childhood. In a sick way, he inspired me to strive for success, and as soon as I could make my own decisions, I left my past behind and never looked back. Acquiring Broussard's company will make my wealth far greater than his. I am half his age. It will destroy him."

His words echoed in her head, and she found herself staring at the scar on his chin. Her voice wavered when she asked, "Is he your stepfather?"

Javier shrugged. She had her answer.

Oh, no.

Her knees weakened, and she plopped down on a nearby wooden bench.

Easton Finn was his stepfather. That was why Javier had looked at her with such disgust. He thought Easton was her lover. Not only did he hate her, but he believed she had slept with the man who had been trying to ruin his life ever since he was a child.

"Javier…I'm sorry. I didn't know." She struggled to lift her voice above a whisper.

"We don't have time for this." He picked up a pair of women's hiking shoes and leaned down. Vivian blinked when he took her shoes off and swiftly worked the hiking shoes onto her feet. "These fit." He stood up again, gathering the items and removing his wallet to pay for them.

He turned his back to her.

"Javier."

"Vivian." It was a command, an order to compose herself. "We will change in the fitting rooms and depart from here."

She followed his lead, and within minutes they had both changed into the outdoor clothes. Javier drove the car to a lot by the woods, and they parked and walked into the woods in silence. The tension suffocated her. As they hiked, her mind raced. She stared at Javier's back encased in an ordinary cotton shirt, the faded jeans that clung to his long legs, and she thought about the terrible truth she had just discovered.

With every step they took, the tightness in her throat increased. It all made sense now. Easton Finn really wanted to destroy Javier—not only to take his merger but to humiliate him, personally and emotionally. And she had been his instrument.

Vivian hated Easton Finn for all he had done to Javier, and she hated herself for being part of it. Yes, there was no way she could have known. She had been doing what she did for Molly, her best friend.

But in no way did that knowledge bring her any relief, because she didn't want to have been the instrument who hurt Javier even more than he'd already been hurt.

She had to set things straight, although she didn't know how she could even begin.

Vivian took a big gulp from her water bottle and wiped the sweat off her forehead with the back of her hand. "Javier, we can't just not talk." She stopped short.

"There's nothing to talk about. You asked me a question, and I answered it. That's all." He came to a halt and looked at her over his shoulder. Then he shook his head, as if thinking to himself, and continued to hike.

She called after him. "You can't honestly expect me to stay quiet about this." Sweat dripped from her neck down her tank top. He didn't respond, and Vivian resumed walking with a deep sigh.

Sun rays slipped from in between long leaves of the tall, arched lime trees, shining down on the bushes. A light breeze swept over her skin, relieving the heat for a moment. She smelled moist earth and tree sap. Anyone else would rave about the outstanding air quality, about what a beautiful day it was to hike outdoors, but it didn't matter to her. The air was heavy and stuffy, which was just how she felt.

She struggled to match Javier's strides. He marched like an athlete, with power and agility.

"Javier, can you please slow down?" she finally asked after an hour of torture.

"Just keep up the pace," he replied without looking back.

"I want to get there alive," she panted. "Is this a punishment?"

"No."

She didn't believe him.

"I swear to you, I didn't know who he was." She said it loud enough to bring Javier to a temporary halt. His back stiffened, his hands stilling alongside his body. "I know it's none of my business, but—"

"It's not," he replied angrily, without looking back.

He strode off again. If anything, he walked even faster.

"You just won't talk to me. Nice." Vivian shook her head. "Well, if training for a marathon is the only way…" she muttered under her breath.

Propelled by an instinct that she could no longer control, she increased her speed, pushing past her own limits. Her heart hammered in her chest, and as she surged forward, gravel flew down the slope beneath her feet.

"Vivian," he shouted as she ran past him. She was past caring.

She ran ahead, cold sweat breaking out on her skin and her mouth dry as her breath came in short pants. She heard him catching up, but she ran as fast as she could.

For a single moment, it was all so simple. Her hair flying in the wind, caressing her face, the threads of light coming through the treetops of the forest…

Javier swore loudly behind her.

She turned to see him hopping on one foot, trying to maintain balance as he clutched the other in both hands.

"What happened?"

He hobbled to a rock and sat down. "My foot hit a rock, and my ankle turned. I didn't see it in my way." He wrinkled his forehead when he removed his shoe and peeled his sock off.

Blood covered the top of his foot, and his toes were already turning purple. Although he tried to breathe normally, there was no doubt he was in a lot of pain.

Vivian's stomach tightened. "Is it broken?" She kneeled down next to him.

"I doubt it," he muttered.

Vivian outlined the bruised and bloodied area very gently with the tips of her fingers. He suppressed a groan.

"You're in pain."

"It's just an ache," he said. "I'll feel better soon."

It was so like Javier to conceal his vulnerability. He was always so strong and in control, she could only imagine that admitting pain and suffering—even if it was only physical suffering—didn't come easily for him.

"You can't keep on hiking."

"What other option do we have? We are three hours away from the bed-and-breakfast and still a couple of hours from the campsite where we should find Laura."

Vivian shook her head. There was no way he could walk for two more hours with his foot bruised and swollen. "Stay right there," she said.

She left to look for help—although of what kind, she wasn't sure.

Javier opened his mouth to call her back, but she disappeared faster than his stock price would fall if he lost the merger.

Gone. She was gone.

She had probably taken off to get the advantage over him. She would find Molly's mother, talk to her, and somehow convince her to say something that would screw him over at the end. By the time Javier found them, it would be too late.

He'd almost believed her frightened eyes when she told him she didn't know Easton was his stepfather. She had never mentioned their relationship to him. It was not as though he considered Easton his stepfather, anyway. Javier hadn't seen the man face-to-face in a very long time, and he had heard that Easton and his mother had divorced nastily years ago.

The thought of Vivian sleeping with Easton and helping him destroy the merger Javier had so carefully crafted made him pound his fist into the ground.

He stood up, shifting his weight to his healthy foot. Pain shot up his leg, although it was nothing compared to the ache in his chest. What felt like over fifteen minutes had passed, and Vivian had not returned. She had betrayed him again.

He wasn't going to stand and wait. Hurt or not, he was going to—

"Javier."

He turned around to see Vivian running his way, panting. Her tank top clung to her sweaty skin, her chest heaving.

She'd come back. He smiled before he could stop himself, and a dangerous combination of warmth and relief filled his heart. She'd come back for him.

Damn her.

"I saw the sign for a bed-and-breakfast only a mile to the south. If you can walk that far, we can go there to get you an ice pack, ibuprofen, and some rest. We might be able to call for help from there."

"I don't need a doctor. I just need to rest," he said.

Vivian picked up the backpack from the ground and closed the gap between them, sliding her arm around his waist.

"Come on, then."

He stepped back. "Vivian, I'm not about to lean on you. I'm too heavy."

"I won't break." She smiled, tightening her arm around his waist. Javier took a deep breath. Her arms were around him, and the top of her head was under his chin. Javier swallowed.

He would make her think she was helping him without overloading her. Shifting his weight to the healthy foot, he leaned on her superficially. Sharp pain shot through his ankle.

Vivian caught on to his plan immediately. "Javier, it's okay. Lean on me." She positioned herself next to him so he could lean on her shoulder for help without exerting himself too much.

He finally accepted her assistance.

When had he last been injured? He didn't want to think about it... It was too long ago. The woman who was supposed to help him then, his mother, had downplayed his pain and asked one of the maids to care for him. The staff members had turned over regularly, never staying long enough to get close to a child who often had unexplained injuries and whose parents traveled a great deal.

He hated for any woman to see him weak. Truth be told, if they had been in the city, there was no way he would have relied on her.

Although the pain remained, something akin to peace blanketed him as they moved through the woods. He focused on the sounds of their clothes rubbing together, the imprint their shoes made on the ground. When he glanced over his shoulder, he saw a light, barely visible circle of dust in their wake.

A voice inside him whispered that dust wasn't the only thing he was leaving behind.

Chapter Ten

Vivian glanced around the timber cottage. It was small but luxurious, with an old-world charm. The big four-poster bed was covered with an elegant bedspread and embroidered pillows, and white rugs accented the dark wood floor. Vintage lamps added to the ambience, casting a soft glow on either side of the bed. Lace curtains framed the window, which unveiled a faraway valley hemmed in by snowcapped mountains.

"I can hold the ice packs myself," Javier said. He shot her an amused look from his position lying on the chaise longue.

"Of course." Vivian folded her arms. "There's not a doctor close by, but the clerk said someone can look at your foot tomorrow."

"I don't need a doctor. The ibuprofen you gave me is kicking in, and these help." He sat up and pointed at the ice packs on his foot and ankle.

Vivian nodded. She walked to the carafe by the bedside table, poured some water into a glass, and drank it in a few big, noisy gulps.

"Do you need anything else?" she asked him, pouring

herself more water.

For one moment, she imagined in his reply. *You. You are all I need.*

No, the thought was foolish. If the past day was anything to go by, all he wanted was for her to be gone. And sadly, not even that realization kept her pulse from racing when he stood up.

"A shower."

"Do you need any help?"

"I'll manage." He had to hop on his good foot, but he reached the bathroom without much difficulty.

A few minutes later, his phone rang on the white dresser. He'd placed it there before he sat. Vivian hadn't given it much thought. She glanced down at it without picking it up and saw the caller ID: Edouard Broussard.

The Frenchman probably wondered if they'd found Molly's mother yet. Or maybe he had news to share with them. Vivian's fingers itched to answer, but she resisted. No more secrets.

When Javier joined her in the room a moment later, he wore only a fluffy towel wrapped around his waist. From the ankle up, the man looked as if nothing had ever been wrong with him.

Vivian blinked, trying to calm her response. How could any woman resist the temptation of approaching him, running her fingers through the damp curls of his chest hair, nuzzling her lips along the curve of his neck, and caressing every bit of his freshly washed body?

"Your phone rang," she said quickly, hoping to take her mind off his body. "It was Edouard."

He arched an eyebrow. "What did he want?"

"I didn't answer."

He rested both hands on his waist for a moment. His eyes fixed nowhere in particular. Then he moved. "Let's find out."

On speakerphone, they explained that finding Laura's mother had become a bigger task than they had expected. Together, the three of them decided that since Laura was going to be at her campsite for another night, a slight delay would be acceptable. Javier and Vivian would spend the night at the cottage and resume their journey in the morning.

Edouard told them Matt Smith had denied having anything to do with hiring men to stalk Molly, as well as any personal involvement with her. Edouard had run a background check on Matt and found nothing. The Frenchman was adamant that finding Laura remained a priority. He didn't want any loose ends, lest the story leak to the press.

After they hung up, Vivian turned to go into the bathroom.

"Thank you," Javier said.

She imagined he thanked her for waiting for him to talk to Edouard.

When she returned wearing a soft robe she had found in the bathroom, she dried her hair with her towel and wondered why he'd really thanked her. Might he be warming up to her? The thought encouraged her to try to talk to him. What could he do, anyway? Run?

A knock sounded at the door, and she opened it. The clerk from reception presented a small tray filled with cold cuts, tea sandwiches, and juices—the food she had ordered when they checked in.

"I'm glad this isn't awkward," she joked, with a glance at the heart-shaped sandwiches. She set the tray on the top of the coffee table, and she and Javier ate in silence.

"Are you feeling any better?" she asked between bites. "You look better."

"I'm good."

"Javier…I have to tell you something."

He bit into an apple. "Isn't this fortunate timing, since I'm stranded?"

She laughed, enjoying the momentary glimpse of the old Javier. Then she sobered, afraid to lose the courage she'd needed to bring up the subject. "I don't know if there will ever be a good time to try to convince you I didn't know Easton was your stepfather and that I never slept with him."

"What difference does it make? In less than twenty-four hours, this will all be sorted, and we won't have to see each other again."

"I don't mind if you hate me for lying to you in the beginning, or for believing my friend. But I can't stand that you think I'd knowingly partner up with the man who destroyed your childhood." Her voice wavered.

"Didn't Molly know? When she first met with him?"

"I don't know. She didn't tell me about him or what she was doing until after it happened and she was fired. I learned most of it all at once."

"Well, don't you wonder why that is? Since you two were close?"

"Perhaps she thought she could do it on her own."

He crossed his arms and assessed her. Vivian wasn't sure if he believed her—or if he liked what he saw. She held the robe closed over her chest when she shifted in her seat.

"My point is, I'm sorry about Easton. But I'm curious… Didn't your mother ever notice your injuries? Didn't she know?"

"I don't want your pity," he said flatly. "Talking about it is pointless."

"Quite the contrary. You have to talk about these things."

He shook his head, avoiding looking at her. "It's all in the past."

"It's part of who you are. The scar on your chin isn't the only one you have," Vivian insisted.

She didn't believe for one second that it was in the past.

When he finally spoke, his accent was pronounced. "She

pretended she didn't know. She didn't think of it as child abuse. Her husband kept saying I needed discipline, and that was how he'd been brought up. So when I had a purple spot on my legs or arms, she just looked away."

Tears filled her eyes. "Did it happen often?" His gaze skimmed her face. Pain hid below the control he was trying so hard to keep. "She should have defended you," Vivian said.

"She was blinded by whatever twisted feelings she had for him. She didn't want to jeopardize her marriage by siding with her son." He stood up.

"I'm so sorry." Vivian moved to embrace him from behind, wrapping her arms around his waist. Thoughts of this man as a young boy being beaten in the household where he should have been safe and nurtured haunted her.

When he tried to disentangle her arms from around him, she only held on tighter, resting her head on his shoulder.

He stiffened, then relaxed for a moment. This time he succeeded in turning around and freeing his arms enough to hold her.

Vivian sniffed. She was a mess, tears flowing down her cheeks as Javier looked down at her. No more contempt shadowed his eyes, no more hidden feelings. A lonely tear made its way down his cheek, but there was something more than sorrow in his eyes. She couldn't quite understand what it was. He stared at her and held her gaze. She didn't dare move.

And then he gently stepped back and moved a few feet away.

"Javier, please…" she started, unsure of what she asked for.

She gazed up at him. He wore a towel around his waist, and she was still in her robe. Yet when she had embraced him, she had been engulfed by the desire to reach to a part of him that he kept hidden from her—though not as deeply as he thought.

Now a different kind of heat flooded her at the sight of his taut nipples, his wide chest, and the tanned, broad shoulders in front of her. Vivian wiped the tears from her eyes with the back of her hand.

If awareness had ever crackled between a man and a woman, she witnessed it at that moment. His eyes raked over her. "I want you, Vivian." His admission sliced through the silence. "That's all I know right now. But I don't know if I can forget all you've done."

Vivian chose to ignore everything after the words *I want you.* She didn't want to talk or to dissect any more old wounds—his or hers. Her eyes skimmed to the bed, her heart thumping. This was it.

"I want you, too, in all sorts of ways."

"Take your robe off," he demanded.

She was more than happy to comply with his request. The softness of the cotton sliding down her skin left a trail of goose bumps behind. Vivian knew the fabric wasn't to blame, but rather Javier's blatant appreciation.

When the robe had pooled at her feet, she raised her eyes to meet his. Heat coiled low in her stomach. She enjoyed watching his Adam's apple bob. The gleam in his eyes. That self-control of his threatening to slip away.

She smiled at the wave of empowerment that swept through her as he closed the short distance between them. Maybe he could just take her up against the wall to give her the release her body craved. Though judging by the way his lips twitched, the heat of his eyes trailing down her figure, Javier had different plans.

Sheer delight coursed through her when their bodies met, skin to skin, man to woman. He lowered his head and branded her mouth in a kiss that was almost violent. Vivian's skin tingled, her hands linked around his neck, her fingertips gliding over his smooth skin. Their tongues swirled together, wrestling.

This kiss tasted not of guilt, not of doubt, not of pain.

He caressed her shoulders, her lower back. Finally his hands cupped her bare bottom, pulling her to him. A tortured gasp escaped her lips when she felt a hard bulge under the towel he still wore.

He shifted his weight slightly from one side to the other, and she managed to tear her lips from his. "Your foot. Is it all right?"

"I don't give a damn about my foot."

With darkened eyes, he smiled at her—the most sensual smile she'd ever seen. She touched his chest, tugging her fingers through the hair and caressing his nipples, making him groan. His towel slipped to the floor and covered her feet.

A glorious feeling beat through her. *He's naked, and all for me.* She touched him, widening her eyes with pleasure when she felt his throbbing cock against her soft belly.

Javier pushed her backward. With a few missteps and stumbles across the room, they reached the bed. She laughed when they plopped down, but amusement washed away when she caught his eyes—his dark, lonely eyes—perusing her with undeniable desire. With lust.

At this point, she didn't care what he offered her. The way her heart raced, the hot tingle between her legs, the raw need that rushed down her body…it all drove her. For this kind of desire, it was worth losing all control.

She wriggled out of his embrace, gesturing for him to lie down. Wearing only a sexy smile, he scooted up the bed with his elbows.

Vivian leaned over him, kissing his neck, tasting his chest. He ran the fingers of one hand through her hair while the other searched for her core. She swayed her hips, making it easier for him. When his fingers brushed against her flesh, she sucked in a breath.

"You are so wet," he said. His accent thickened the way it always did when he wanted her.

His touch just felt too good, his fingers stretching her walls, exploring deep inside her. If he continued at this rate, she would come in no time and completely lose track of her goal. It was time to drive him insane for once...or twice, if she was lucky. *As many times as this last night with him will allow...*

She couldn't resist bucking against him one more time, and the movement put her right on the edge. With a sigh, she slowly retreated, moving down his body. He muttered something in Spanish, adding to her arousal.

"Enough, Vivian." He propped himself up on his elbows. "I want to taste you."

"Good things come to those who wait," she said with a strangled chuckle. She licked his thick thigh while her hand cupped him. She loved how he tensed.

When she raised her head, her eyes found his.

"If you continue at this rate, there won't be much waiting," he warned her.

She licked his needy shaft. It swelled even more, and he moaned. She took him in her mouth, her lips sliding across the warm, velvety skin. Her teeth grazed over him before she glided her tongue over his cock and began to suck all of him.

Then, without warning, he lifted her from him. She sat on him, legs spread on either side of his, feeling insanely hot. Insanely ready.

He stretched out his arm and reached for his wallet inside the bedside drawer. He took a condom out and ripped the foil square open with such urgency, she worried he would tear it apart. Still on top of him, she wrapped her legs around his waist. As he closed the space between them, his skin on her skin, his mouth hovering over hers, a throaty sound escaped her lips.

Javier put the condom on, and her fingers ached to touch him. He placed his hands beneath her hips, brought her closer, and thrust inside her. She moved along with his rhythm, wondering how long she would be able to stand the warm ripples of pleasure beginning to form. He thrust into her hard and fast a few times, then she sucked in her breath when he took all of his shaft out, only to penetrate her again even deeper. Even stronger.

Her brain lost the ability to keep up with her body, which needed release, and soon. He kissed her, a passionate kiss that lasted longer than she could bear. When he pinched her nipples, a long, intoxicating wave of pleasure washed through every part of her body.

At the end, it was like a double act on a trapeze, where they had successfully balanced, swung, and danced—with the exception that all they had was each other. No bars. No ropes. No safety nets. And they had made it.

Vivian reached for another strawberry and slid it between her lips, still tender from being kissed. She refused to look at the clock, knowing that her time with Javier was coming to an end. In between dozing and making love, she hadn't left his side. They'd showered together, eaten together, and made love with such passion, she ached just remembering.

Vivian shook her head. It wasn't time for thinking. Not just yet.

From her position on her stomach beside him, her chin propped on her hands, she glanced at Javier's glorious body sprawled on the bed beside her. A satisfied smile played over his lips.

"What is it?" he asked.

She said the first thing that came to mind. "How did you

get to be so successful? I mean, didn't you say you left home? I was just wondering."

His slight frown and the surprise in his eyes indicated she had said the wrong thing.

"I was always good with numbers. I studied economics at university, and my first goal was to work at every opportunity I was given. I wanted to repay my mother for paying for my studies. She didn't want me to, but I insisted, because the money came from him." Bitterness laced his voice, the hatred he felt for his stepfather coming through.

"I joined a finance group as an intern, started to work my way up, learned about stocks, and soon I had enough contacts to find investors for my own business." He swallowed. "I paid them. I don't owe them anything."

"It's hard for you to see your mother, isn't it?" She remembered the awkward run-in at the ball.

He reached over and stroked the length of her back. "She thinks because they divorced that none of it ever happened."

Vivian thought of her loving mother and her doting stepfather, who had done the best he could for his new family. She wished she could take away the sadness of the little boy who still lived inside Javier and replace his childhood memories with better ones. "Do you miss her?"

"No." His fingers made invisible circles on her back.

She ignored the currents of heat traveling through her body and embraced the warmth of this rare moment of shared intimacy. "I miss my parents."

"Is that why you have those nightmares?" His hot palm closed on her lower back, the gentle tap of his fingers encouraging her to keep talking.

"I haven't had them for a long time. I guess after Molly's death and being away from home… I dream of them going away in a car and not coming back. Even when I run after them and call them from the street, they just look at me in slow motion and keep driving away."

Javier's arms tightened around her, wrapping her as if he wanted to protect her from her sad thoughts.

A new awareness tugged at her heart.

She had broken the promise she'd made to her mother never to look for her biological father, and that had ended in an even worse heartbreak. She'd wondered, for years, if maybe her father had changed his mind about her. After her mother's death, it had made sense to reach out to him, but she'd been terribly disappointed. He had turned out to be indifferent to her, and even a bit bothered by her looking for him.

Could that be the reason for her nightmares? Were they about the promise she'd broken to her parents, and her conflicted feelings about the vow she'd made after Molly's death?

"Enough thinking," he said. His fingers ran through her hair, and when they began to massage her scalp, all the tension inside her melted.

"The tea is lovely."

Javier simply nodded, stirring his black coffee in the small white cup as he looked anywhere but in her eyes. Since waking up, he had avoided her. He'd used the bathroom before she was out of bed and left for the restaurant a few minutes ahead of her.

Now he focused on the space above her shoulder as he bit into his toast. Vivian turned around to see what he was looking at. There was nothing but the flowery wallpaper of a virtually empty restaurant.

It was as if he had carefully engineered this distance to make it hard for her to talk to him. Watching the way his long fingers outlined the coffee cup, the way the tight black shirt clung to his muscles, made her fingers ache with wanting to touch him.

"Are you done?" He glanced at his watch.

"Yes." *Not if I can help it.*

She followed him out, covering a yawn. Only when they had returned to hiking toward Laura's campsite did she speak to him again. "Javier, you've been silent all morning. What's wrong?"

"I'm focusing on getting to the right place," he said in a clipped tone. Although he had refused to see a doctor, Javier had taken another ibuprofen this morning. She could tell by the way he moved and his slower pace that his foot was still bothering him.

"You don't have to be monosyllabic. I asked you what the time was earlier, and you didn't respond."

"It's nine o'clock."

"It doesn't matter now. My point was, I get it that you can't wait to be rid of me, but you don't have to be hostile."

"Hostile," he repeated with sarcasm, his head tilting from side to side as if he didn't believe what he was hearing.

"Since it'll be all over soon, why keep trying, right? Why try to make it civilized?" Perhaps he wanted to make sure she didn't expect any more than he was willing to give. He was done with her, and instead of letting her down easily, he'd chosen the more effective route of trying to drive her away.

"You think I'm avoiding you because I don't want you anymore."

"It makes sense, doesn't it?"

She had barely finished speaking when he slammed her against a thick tree trunk and closed the gap between them. Vivian gasped.

"*You* are what's wrong with me, Vivian," he said. There was an unveiled intensity in his dark eyes. "I can't stop wanting you."

Swiftly, Javier leaned in and kissed her hard, almost as if in punishment. She fought to breathe, raising trembling fingers to his chest. His heartbeat matched hers. He looked down at her, his eyes blazing with desire, his deep gaze a promise and a challenge. He wanted her surrender. She linked her arms around his neck as she almost stumbled, her knees weak and shaky with yearning. Javier only embraced her tighter.

"I've got you," he told her, and she didn't know exactly what he meant. What she knew was that right or wrong, guilty or free, she wanted—no, *needed*—him.

"Come." He guessed her thoughts, took her hands in his and led her deeper into the woods. Although it didn't take him long to find a quiet spot where the trees arched closer together and boulders created a bit more privacy, for her the minutes went on forever.

Chapter Eleven

The thump of the backpack falling to the earth let her know he'd found the right spot against a heavy tree trunk. They were alone in the middle of the woods in daylight…about to make love.

An escalating quiver spread through her body when his fingers unbuttoned her jeans.

"Clothes off," he demanded, squatting down to remove her panties and jeans. He got to his feet. Taken over by an instinct that was new to her, she raised her arms up so he could take her tank top off.

She glanced around once again, but a blackbird singing in a nearby tree was their only witness.

Javier pulled her bra aside. His fingers found her painfully hard nipples. Propping her against the tree trunk, he lifted her from the ground as she wrapped her legs around him. She noticed how he sucked in his breath and suppressed a groan. Was he in pain? Her lips parted to ask him, but he kissed her, nibbling on her lower lip as his tongue swirled with hers. She matched his urgency, her fingers splayed on his large chest, her thumbs caressing his nipples through his shirt. If his foot still hurt, he didn't care. She saw in his eyes that all he wanted was to bury himself inside her.

"Javier, please," she begged. Her fingers dipped down to his waist, outlining his bulge and sending a wave of heat through her system.

He found her entrance and thrust inside her, pumping so hard that they both moaned. Vivian hugged him as tight as she could. He held her at her waist, moving his powerful shaft in and out of her, making her insane with desire as the tree branches swayed overhead and the blackbird took flight.

Javier increased his speed, and soon she moaned louder. An overwhelming climax burst inside her, overpowering her, and she bit her lip to keep from screaming his name out loud in the middle of the woods. His pleasure followed hers, and they both collapsed to the ground.

Vivian could have stayed there forever, with Javier still semi-erect and pulsating inside of her, their bodies linked, her head resting on his shoulder. But the forest had other plans. A group of ants tickled behind her leg, and she moved, shaking the ants away. Javier stood and pulled his pants up.

The sound of his zipper reminded her she was stark naked, and embarrassment heated her cheeks.

What had just happened? She had never given herself to someone with such abandonment and need in any setting, let alone a public place.

Javier looked around them and leaned down to retrieve her clothes. Her jeans, her top, her bra...her panties, for goodness' sake! He deposited all these items in her lap without daring to face her, then offered his hand to help her stand up.

Vivian rose to her feet, avoiding looking at him, and put her clothes on as quickly as her trembling fingers could manage.

"I apologize," he said under his breath. She smoothed her top down with her hands and met his disappointed eyes. "It wasn't my plan to take you like this. I lost control."

Vivian simply nodded, faking a strong front as her mind worked overtime to assess what had happened. She supposed he had taken the easy way out. He'd taken her in the wilderness, hot and intense, and then apologized. The apology unsettled her as much as it surprised her.

She couldn't keep her mind from racing.

I want you in my life, Vivian, he had said the previous day. Somehow, in the tumult of everything that had happened since then, his proposal had vanished from her brain.

They returned to their hike, Javier leading at a slightly slower pace. It was easier for her to follow now, yet she preferred to stay a couple of steps behind him. She had too much on her mind to face him now.

After a long hour of silent walking, she spoke, blurting out her question before she could lose her courage. "What did you mean when you said to me the other day that you wanted me in your life?"

Javier's body stiffened, and he stopped walking. Vivian held her breath, waiting for him to turn and answer, but he strode off without speaking.

"I'm not asking if the offer still stands," she called. "I was only curious about what you meant."

"I thought we could explore this attraction. I would have set you up with a nice flat in London. We could have gone on trips, taken in shows, and enjoyed each other's company," he replied.

Vivian frowned. "I already live in London. Why would you set me up with a flat?"

"Because you could live somewhere nicer and closer to my office, giving me easier access when I am in town."

Of course. His proposal—even before he had hated her

as he did now, hated how she made him feel—had always been surface-deep. She would be his modern concubine, one of many.

Vivian crossed her arms defensively. "You wanted me to be your mistress."

"That's not how I see it."

"I suppose it doesn't matter how you see it. It wouldn't have worked out." She gave him a dismissive shrug. "I could never be satisfied being one of the many women you have at your beck and call."

"I doubt there will be more than one of you." His voice was flat, yet when her eyes met his, she saw a fleeting touch of sadness.

Vivian shook her head. *Enough with imagining things.* "Somehow I don't take that as a compliment."

His hand tightened around the strap of the backpack. "Take it as you like." He strode off again, and she followed.

Soon, they approached the campsite. The tall trees gave way to smaller bushes and more colorful vegetation. Groups of hikers and campers strolled through the park, some taking pictures. The soft breeze caressing her face did nothing to relieve her anxiety.

"Can you see her?" Javier asked.

Vivian glanced around, paying more attention to the faces. She was about to say no when a petite brunette in her fifties emerged from a tent.

Vivian pointed. "I see her."

"And that's why we've come." As Javier finished explaining, he raised his smartphone close to Laura's face to record their conversation. "We wanted your take on what happened. I sent money to cover her funeral arrangements through my office, but I have never spoken to you before."

They sat on rocks apart from Laura's friends. Vivian wrung her hands. "I'm sorry to surprise you like this," she said. "It must have been hard for you. You left England so quickly after the funeral."

Laura Richardson crossed her arms, a self-protective gesture. "Molly and I didn't share everything," she said after a long silence. "We didn't have the typical mother-daughter relationship. But she always came to me when she was in trouble."

"Is there a chance she invented the threats against her?" Javier asked.

"No. She was in trouble." Laura sighed. "Molly always enjoyed the nice things in life. She often got into debt and dipped into her savings account. But when her debt increased and Roger—I mean Easton Finn—offered her money to get some information to him, she took the opportunity."

She accepted money?

"So this wasn't revenge against Javier, like she told me," Vivian said.

She lied to me.

"She didn't mean to deceive you, Vivian. She just didn't want you to know how deep in league with Roger she was." Laura gave her a sympathetic smile. "As she started to work for you, Javier, I guess she became involved with you, and that affected her task."

"How so?" Javier asked.

"She told me she had the opportunity to give Easton some important numbers, but she began to question what she was doing."

The blood drained from Vivian's face, and a chill formed in the pit of her stomach. "Easton got mad at her then," she said. "Frustrated. I bet he hired the men to stalk her."

Javier's tight nod echoed her suspicion.

"Laura, do you think Molly would have killed herself?" Javier asked.

"I dwelled on it a lot. No mother wants to bury her own daughter." Laura blinked back tears. "That's not how it's supposed to happen."

"Will you fly back to London and talk to the police? If you tell them what you know, we can try to look for security tapes from Molly's building to see if we can identify the men who followed her, or if Easton came inside her apartment the night she died. Maybe her former neighbors know something. Since the police ruled it a suicide so quickly, they might have missed something."

Laura's eyes widened. "Do you think there's a chance she was...murdered?"

"I don't know," Javier said. "But if she really was bullied into suicide, someone will pay for it."

"I'll fly to London." Laura stood up. "I'll do whatever it takes."

And with that statement, the wheels got in motion quickly. Javier called for a helicopter, and the three of them hiked back to the bed-and-breakfast, which was near the closest area it could land safely to pick them up.

A wide range of emotions darted at Vivian's heart long after the conversation had ended. Resentment at her friend for not trusting her the way she should have. Relief at the way Javier was acting, making it his mission to make the responsible party pay for Molly's death. Pain, because she knew deep inside that once this all came to an end, Javier would walk out of her life.

One more person she loved who would leave her.

Her parents. Her biological father. Molly.

Molly. Now more than ever, Vivian wanted closure.

During the time it took for a helicopter to appear to take them all to Zurich, Vivian thought about what she would say.

Finding the right words was hard, especially considering that Javier would not look at her. He stood with his arms crossed, gazing at the vast infinitude of green and at the mountains.

His profile was hard and unsmiling.

I owe him a proper apology.

A lesser man might have been happy that he had secured his merger, regardless of the cost. But Javier wasn't the cold individual he pretended to be.

They landed on the tarmac in Zurich, only to board his private jet immediately. Javier and Vivian went on to Paris to meet with Edouard as planned. Laura was sent on a direct flight to London, where she would go to the police early the next morning. She seemed determined to do whatever she could to help. Vivian understood that Laura had been too caught up in her feelings of loss and guilt to imagine that Molly's death had been caused by anything other than suicide.

Javier made a few phone calls, pulled a few strings, and got in touch with a criminal lawyer. He also asked his investigator to find security tapes from Molly's building and the nearby cross streets, businesses, and ATMs, any of which might have caught footage of Easton or the two men.

On the jet to Paris, they were alone for the first time since that hour in the woods. Vivian's anxiety grew, but it wasn't until Javier chose a leather chair a couple of rows away from hers that she knew for certain he was avoiding her at any cost.

After takeoff, she unbuckled her seat belt and moved to the empty seat beside his.

"Javier, first of all, I want to thank you for doing this." She watched him, holding her breath as his gaze drifted from his magazine to her face.

"I have my own interest, too. If Easton is guilty. I'm no saint."

"I still say thank you. I'm sorry I've delayed your merger, and that I thought you were this horrible person." She swallowed. "After my mother and stepfather died, I looked for my biological father. When I was a child, my mother made me promise never look for him. But I needed to connect with someone, I felt so alone, and I broke that promise. I looked for him, and he couldn't have cared less about me." Vivian pulled the words from deep inside. "With Molly's death…I wanted her to be avenged, yes. But I've realized I also wanted to follow through with a promise that involved someone else."

"Vivian—" he started, but she put her hand over his and continued.

"I'm truly sorry for compromising your merger. I hope you still get it."

She looked down. Her hand was caught in his, and a wave of awareness traveled up her arm and through the rest of her body. Javier clasped her hand tight, his eyes on hers, but when she thought he was about to lean down to kiss her, he withdrew his hand. Pressing his lips together, he returned his attention to the magazine.

"I know you are sorry, Vivian. But that doesn't change anything."

It doesn't change anything.

Of course.

The words stayed with Vivian, hammering in her brain as they left the jet and traveled by car to the Broussard office, where she sat opposite the old man across the antique table.

Javier stood, arms crossed, leaning against a floor-to-ceiling shelf stacked with leather-bound books. While the recording played for Edouard, the only voice she heard was Javier's.

It doesn't change anything.

But the words didn't make sense.

A part of her couldn't believe she was just another woman in his life. They had made love, he had savagely taken her in the woods in the morning after declaring he couldn't stop wanting her.

Could everything that had passed between them really have been about the merger? Now that he'd gotten what he wanted, she was of no use?

"I definitely have enough to proceed with the merger." Edouard's clipped voice brought her back to reality.

She glanced over her shoulder at Javier. A glint of satisfaction flashed in his eyes, but he didn't smile.

"Thank you, Edouard," Vivian said. "You sending us off to meet Laura helped us to fit the pieces of the puzzle together."

"I'm glad. According to Javier, the wheels are in motion to figure out what happened to Molly. Let us hope the prosecutors will find enough evidence to file charges against Easton."

"They will," Javier said from behind her.

"I'm also glad you didn't close the deal with Easton," Vivian added.

Edouard chuckled. "I never seriously considered him. I don't appreciate his business ethics." He glanced at Javier. "Or his personal ethics."

"But then why?" Vivian asked.

"It got you running, didn't it?" He smiled. "I always believed in Javier. Nevertheless, if there was a thread of doubt that could harm my foundation or legacy, it needed to be chased down."

"I'm sorry for any inconvenience I've caused," Vivian said.

Edouard stood up, his face unreadable. Unsure, she followed his cue, wondering if he would throw her out of his office. It seemed possible.

"Vivian, you are a loyal friend, and you did what you thought was right," Edouard said gently, his features softening. A part of her wanted to cling to the instant relief pouring through her, while another warned her it was too soon.

Edouard reached over and embraced her, the kind gesture causing tears to fill her eyes. She held him back with more than an appropriate amount of enthusiasm, pressing her lips together and closing her eyes to keep the tears from rolling down her flushed cheeks.

Funny that although she could count on one hand the times she'd met Edouard, a sense of belonging suffused her as they bid farewell.

"I'm glad I had the opportunity to meet you." Edouard patted her back when she straightened up and wiped at her tears. "I admire brave hearts. If we only acted on what had been proven right, we wouldn't ever achieve anything or try new things."

"Thank you." Edouard had a point…

Javier cleared his throat.

"Don't you agree?" Edouard turned to Javier, who had his arms lazily crossed over his broad chest and a face as hard as marble. He made no verbal response. There was only the enigmatic glint flashing in his eyes. Edouard shook his head in disapproval and asked Vivian, "Will you be all right, my dear?"

Her lips formed a tremulous smile. She didn't know how to reply. From now on, her life would never be the same, on so many levels. She knew she needed to make a complete assessment of her past and present, to analyze her actions and the reasons behind them. She could barely begin to think about it now. Within the course of a few days, her whole life had changed—the friend she thought she knew, the man she had met and fallen in love with, the possible legal repercussions of what she had done.

After all, Edouard's understanding and generosity were one thing. But how about Javier's? He had been silent about possible implications.

"I'll be fine," Vivian said simply, wishing she could believe her own choked words.

"I have to make some calls," Edouard said. "Javier, could you please show Vivian out?"

"It will be my pleasure." Javier's voice dripped with sarcasm.

Javier held the door open for her and led the way. The beige walls of the hallway seemed to become narrower and narrower. Vivian felt a lump of heat traveling all the way from her knotted stomach up to her throat.

I have to do something. This is my last chance.

"My jet will take you back to London," Javier said as they approached the elevators. "When you reach the lobby, the driver will be waiting for you. Your belongings will be in the car."

Vivian mumbled a thank-you, her palms dampening. She stared at the closed elevator doors. They were on the top floor, and it would take a few moments for the elevator to arrive.

"Human Resources will contact you and take care of whatever dues are owed to you," he continued.

Her job… In the middle of all the changes of the past several hours, her job as a receptionist hadn't even entered her mind. She'd only applied for it because of her desire for revenge. She had other plans for her career, anyway.

She gathered that Javier didn't plan to take any legal action as retaliation for the delay in his merger. Yet her termination had a far stronger implication. He wouldn't trust her to work for him, and she understood that. But it also meant she wasn't going to see him anymore.

No more Javier, not even from behind a reception desk.

No more kissing his tantalizing, full lips.

No more talking and sharing with him about things from her past, things that had made her feel unappreciated and singled out until she had heard herself speak them aloud and begun to question them.

"Javier." His name slipped from her parted lips before she knew what she would say. She swung around to face him.

Javier arched an eyebrow.

Vivian took in the sight of his intriguing black eyes, his granite-like features, his provocative full lips closed. He appeared calm and unstressed.

Look at him, Vivian, because after this moment, he'll only be a haunting memory and a face printed in the newspapers for you.

Would he forget her quickly?

The elevator halted at the floor with a tone that put her senses on full alert.

She glanced at the empty space inside, with its rail and mirror in the middle and no one to take anywhere.

She looked at Javier, who remained standing beside her. He could have shown her to the elevators and left, but he stood…and waited. He stood by her side, and that had to count for something. Maybe this was her time to be vulnerable, just as he had in confiding in her about his past.

I won't leave Paris without trying.

Overwhelmed by everything she wanted to say, she closed the distance between them.

He didn't move.

Vivian stared at his firmly shut lips, his implacable features. He looked down at her, and his thick eyelashes nearly covered his eyes, concealing whatever emotion was hidden behind them. She inhaled his minty, masculine scent one last time.

Before she could change her mind, she covered his lips with hers, her arms wrapping around his neck the same way they had when he had been the one initiating their kisses. The feel of his body, his heat trapped under his clothes, and the passion pulsating in her veins encouraged her to run her tongue across his upper lip.

He didn't react.

She rubbed her lips on his. He suppressed a groan.

"I love you," Vivian whispered close to his mouth, stripping herself bare.

She…loved him? The realization hit her with the force of an emotional slap.

There was no more denying it to herself. The attraction she had at first found disturbing had turned into a torrid passion and now into a love that made her heart tighten with pain every time she thought about parting from him.

How would she go on without seeing him? How had she allowed a man she barely knew to affect her this much?

Well, in her defense, she hadn't. She'd tried to put up a wall, to constantly remind herself that they sought different things, that he was not the man for her.

Just her luck, none of it had worked.

Instead, the midnight-eyed Spanish hunk had found a way to conquer her heart, and he'd stirred up intense emotions, long-forgotten memories, and now this wrenching pain faced with the end of something that could never be.

For he hadn't done it on purpose. Winning her love had never been a part of his plan. Her body, yes. Yet he had her love and didn't know it.

Well, he knows it now.

She felt more exposed than she had when they had made love in the woods, and fully aware she was probably making a fool of herself. But she would be a bigger fool if she didn't. For she loved him—the man who had suffered, who had questioned, and who had made a new life for himself.

Her smile died as soon as he tore himself from her and motioned for her to get in the elevator.

"I can't do this." A blend of urgency, frustration, and anger laced his voice, and his expression was determined. He sighed as if he couldn't wait for the awkwardness to be over.

Vivian pressed her trembling lips together. It took an outstanding effort not to fall apart in front of him. Somehow the message must have made it to her brain, because with a strength she couldn't claim as her own, her feet took a step back, then another, and there she was, inside the elevator, her blurred vision focused on the man she couldn't have.

He can't do this? Or he doesn't want to do this? Or just not with me?

"Good-bye, Vivian Foster." His voice was barely above a whisper, and his black eyes didn't leave hers for a moment as the heavy doors closed between them.

Chapter Twelve

Javier ended his teleconference to China and took a deep breath as he turned off his computer monitor. It was only 1:00 p.m., although it felt much later. Not because of all he had accomplished, but rather because of how little sleep he'd had.

Infierno!

He had tried to forget her.

A week had passed since he'd seen her, and neither working himself to exhaustion nor exercising as if he were training for a triathlon had managed to evict Vivian Foster from his head. Every time he was about to congratulate himself for not thinking about her, he'd realize that he was indeed thinking of her—that her wavy, luscious hair, her endless legs, and those big blue eyes were so fresh in his memory, he could do a mental sketch of her anytime he wanted. And he did... often.

He ran his fingers through his hair.

Taking a gorgeous Italian model out to dinner hadn't helped at all. Somewhere between sitting down in the restaurant and getting the bill, he'd grown bored and lied, saying he had to go, and smoothly turned down an invitation for coffee at her apartment. Lying to himself, though, was a different matter.

She'd lied to him. She'd betrayed him and let him down, and still he would do anything to see her, to bury himself in her curves, to lose all control with her again. Just once.

"Mr. Rivera." His secretary's voice through the intercom interrupted his fantasizing. "My son's day care just called. He's running a high fever, and I might need to drive him to my sister's for the rest of the day. May I take a longer lunch break?"

"Why don't you take the rest of the day off?" he suggested. "Go stay with your son."

"Thank you, sir," she answered. "Before I go, Monsieur Broussard wants you to call him immediately."

Javier made the call, and midway through the conversation Edouard asked whether he would be attending one of his foundation parties. Javier was about to turn the invitation down due to his hectic schedule when Edouard said, "I understand. I was just telling Vivian how hard you work and that I imagined you couldn't make it."

"Vivian?" A frisson ran down his spine. "You've been talking to her?"

"Yes, we keep in touch. I offered for her to come and help me sell some artwork for fund-raising purposes, and she's considering it."

"How is she?"

"She's good." Edouard's short answer intrigued him even further. It was obvious that Vivian had developed some kind of friendship with the older man. But Javier wasn't about to swallow his pride and beg for any snippet of information about her he could get.

It didn't matter. He wasn't going.

"More champagne, Monsieur?" asked the uniformed waitress.

Javier shook his head, his fingers tapping on the glass he had held for what felt like forever. He shouldn't have come.

But he'd had to. He'd pondered the difficult decision for two long weeks until it finally became clear to him that the only alternative to losing his mind would be to attend the function. How bad could it be, seeing her?

Not knowing how she would react had tipped the scale. Would she run to him? Would she treat him with disdain? Or, worse, would she act as if they were old friends and be completely immune to him, as if he didn't matter?

He looked around. The stuffiness of the silent auction party crept into his blood, and his heart rate increased every time he glanced at the large french doors, hoping Vivian would walk in.

Two hours into the auction, he was burning with frustration. She wasn't coming.

He searched for Edouard, and when he found him, he couldn't resist asking about Vivian. The older man told him she had changed her mind.

"Why don't you go and find her?" Edouard suggested gently, his eyes full of sympathy.

Javier snorted. "It's too late."

"My dear friend, it's never too late. You don't have to impose unhappiness upon yourself only because you had no control over the beginning of your affair."

"She told me she loved me at the very end. She couldn't have meant it." Javier spoke his thoughts out loud, staring at the gardens where people were mingling with hors d'oeuvres after the auction.

"Why not? Are you unworthy of her love? You never say much about your past." Edouard gave him a questioning look, and Javier stiffened. "I gather from malicious gossip and common sense that you didn't get what you deserved growing up."

"I don't want to discuss this."

"You don't. Nobody does. But let me tell you this, the beginning doesn't dictate the end. You can have the end of your choosing."

Javier scanned the elegantly dressed guests, who chatted away about the paintings and objets d'art as uniformed waiters served them fine champagne and exquisite appetizers. "She was never supposed to come," he said to Edouard.

"She told me she couldn't," Edouard admitted, scratching his beard with a mischievous smile.

"Why did you tell me she would be here?"

"Because you needed to come to feel how empty your life is without her." Edouard sobered. "I lost my wife and then my daughter, and I found out the hard way. I don't want you to lose her just because of your pride."

Edouard returned to his other guests.

"Sneaky old man," Javier mumbled.

The words echoed in his head. *The beginning doesn't dictate the end. You can have the end of your choosing.*

If he could choose, what choice would he make?

Maybe a part of him was jealous because Vivian's devotion toward Molly was something he'd wanted from his mother—or at least her attention to the abuse he'd suffered. As a child, he had yearned for an advocate, for someone who cared deeply enough to fight for him, to take him from his misery and show him what happiness was. Then he'd grown and become self-sufficient, and such cravings had disappeared.

Self-reliance was a much safer bet.

Vivian had brought old ghosts to life in a way he hadn't expected. And after discovering what she had done for Molly…he hadn't wanted to believe at first. The idea of someone putting everything on the line for a friend didn't make any sense.

Anger and frustration had overtaken him when little by little he'd started to realize that yes, Vivian wasn't perfect. She had lied to him and deceived him at first. She was stubborn, and once she got something in that little head of hers, she saw it through, regardless of the cost. Yes, Vivian Foster was nowhere near perfect…but he loved her anyway.

The realization hit him like a punch to his stomach.

I love her.

He pulled his mobile from his pocket and stabbed at the numbers. "I need the jet now. We're going to London."

Bail denied to entrepreneur Easton Finn. Vivian read the headline on the news Web site before turning off her sleek computer and sliding down from the tall stool. Jennifer, the chatty blond employee, had already logged off and seemed to be looking for her car keys in her bag.

Vivian had gone to the police a couple of times and had told the lawyers she would testify if needed. Helping any way she could gave her a sense of purpose, though she doubted her testimony would be instrumental. They had far better evidence—the confessions of the men who had stalked Molly, identified by security tapes, along with Easton's fingerprints. Easton had killed Molly himself, out of what they assumed was fear that she would come clean to everyone, as she had threatened to do. He hadn't wanted the whole world to know what a bastard he was.

And now they did.

Vivian smiled.

She looked around with satisfaction. The spacious and airy art gallery she managed was new, and it had already become a hit. The weekly exhibit featured a Paris theme. The oil paintings on the walls captured off-the-beaten-track gems from the City of Light.

She'd thought that starting a new job would help her begin a new chapter of her life. Truth was, she still felt like the high-wire artist who had fallen from the ropes with no safety net underneath: broken and embarrassed, filled with pain that went far beyond the physical.

After a lot of soul-searching, she'd made her peace with what had happened to Molly and had even visited her grave. She understood now that her friend had loved her, and if Molly had left the fine print out of her story to Vivian, it hadn't been for lack of trust. She'd done it for her own reasons.

People weren't always what they seemed. Even Laura, Molly's mom, had gained much respect from Vivian after returning to London and fighting to reopen her daughter's case. Everyone deserved a second chance.

Everyone but me.

She didn't want to be bitter. But how could she believe she would ever love someone again when every corner of her heart was fully occupied by the man who had coldly turned his back on her and shut her out of his life?

"You can go. I'll close it," she said to Jennifer, who was about to lock up.

"Thanks. 'Night, Vivian."

"Good night."

Vivian picked up her purse and leaned down to punch the password to set the security alarm on the pad located under the countertop when she heard the door swing open.

"How can I help—" she started, standing up to face the potential customer.

Her mouth went dry in an instant. She blinked a couple of times when her eyes blurred at the sight of tall, broad-shouldered man in a light gray suit and dark shirt.

"Javier…" Her voice trembled.

He looked as imposing and attractive as she remembered him. Her heartbeat escalated, threatening to find a way out of her dark-red silk blouse.

His eyes caught hers and held them captive. Even drawing a deep breath proved difficult. She needed all the oxygen in the room.

"What are you doing here?" she asked after a moment.

"I need to talk to you."

She leaned on the glass top of her desk for support, trying to appear casual.

I can't survive having the ground beneath me torn away once more.

"How did you find me?"

"Edouard told me where you worked." His eyes darted to the paintings hanging on the brick wall. "Paris."

Vivian came out from behind the desk, smoothing her black skirt with her hands in order to dry the cold sweat breaking out on her palms. Edouard. Of course. She had chatted on the phone with the Frenchman a couple of times, and he had insisted she help him with his silent auction, but she had pulled out in the end. The possibility of meeting Javier had frightened her too much.

The auction…wasn't it today?

"Weren't you supposed to be at Edouard's auction?"

His eyes returned to her, skimming over her face. There was something about him, a lightness she wasn't used to seeing in him.

"I was at Edouard's auction," Javier replied. His accent had thickened. "Now I'm here…with you."

"Ah. Well, what do you want from me?"

With only two short steps, he was in front of her, and she could see the dark shadows under his eyes.

"I want you," he said boldly, a smile on his full lips.

Although the surprise of his words made her heart thump erratically and a familiar heat pool low in her stomach, she remained still. Vivian cleared her throat, the memory of their last moments together flashing in her mind. The hurt had stayed with her. "After our last meeting, I thought you wanted nothing to do with me."

"I had to say that, Vivian. At that moment, when you said you loved me, I felt a loss of control greater than when I thought I had lost the merger. I'm not used to feeling like this."

"I thought it had to do with Molly."

"That would have been a great excuse, yes, but I think it had stopped being about Molly. In a way, of course, I wanted you to believe me. But to learn that you would put everything on the line for a friend also fascinated me, though I wouldn't admit it at the time."

"It did?"

"The woods were a big eye-opener for me. I couldn't be around you without wanting you. It exhilarated me, but it also scared me," Javier confessed, lifting his finger to outline her jaw.

Vivian quivered at the familiar touch.

"Remember when I injured my foot and you asked me to lean on you to get to the bed-and-breakfast? That was the first time I had ever let a woman take care of me. You took me to the cottage, nursed me, and even though we didn't see things the same way, you let me make love to you. That night, deep down, I knew I wasn't the same anymore."

"What are you saying?" Vivian asked. Her emotions were a mess, as though a palette of bold, bright colors had been thrown on a white canvas all at once.

"I love you," he declared. He pulled her against him and kissed her once, softly.

"You...you love me?"

"The merger didn't make sense without you. This last month has been hell. All I could think of was you. I am so sorry for hurting you, *mi querida*, and I want to spend the rest of my days making you happy."

"But in the woods…after we made love, the way—"

"I was disappointed in myself for lacking control and taking you like that," Javier replied. "I saw you blushing and gathered you were also disappointed in me. *Infierno*, I tried everything to get over you, Vivian. I've tried being cold, rude, distant… I can't run from what I carry with me." He placed her hand over his chest.

Vivian felt the quickened beating of his heart and cupped his handsome face, murmuring against his lips, "I love you, too."

"Prove it." The challenge in his eyes sent a tremor up her spine. "Marry me. I won't let you go."

Marry him? Vivian's heart jolted, a thrill of pure happiness running through her. Tears of joy rose in her eyes as a strong sense of belonging blanketed her.

"Say yes," he whispered in her ear, and she didn't notice he had walked her into the back room until Javier lifted her up onto a counter. Her body instantly molded to his.

"Yes," she moaned.

He backed off for a second, a serious look on his face. "Yes to the lovemaking or to my marriage proposal?"

"Yes to everything." She kissed him, wrapping her arms around him tightly and knowing she wouldn't let him get away, either. *Ever.*

Acknowledgments

To Entangled, thank you for welcoming me into your awesome team. I'll always be grateful to Alethea Spiridon Hopson for believing in my potential.

To my lovely, ruthless, surprisingly unassuming editor, Ruth Homrighaus. I'm fascinated by your talent and professionalism. If you ever need a kidney donor or a surrogate, give me a call.

Thanks to Yvette Savage for your endless support and enthusiasm.

Thank you Reader, for allowing me to share Vivian and Javier's story with you.

About the Author

Carmen Falcone learned at an early age that fantasizing about fictional characters and places beat doing math homework any day. After she achieved a B.A. in tourism in her hometown in Brazil, she traveled the world and was soon invited to work in Texas, where she met her Swiss husband. She'd always dreamed of becoming a published writer, and after her daughter was born, she revisited that dream of writing–this time, unwilling to give it up. She lives in Austin and enjoys reading, traveling, and spending time with her family and three high-energy pugs. She also loves to procrastinate, so please drop her a line on Twitter or Facebook. Visit Carmen at her website: www.carmenfalcone.com.

Discover more romance from Entangled Indulgence...

Over Her Wed Body
a novel by Alexia Adams

Beckett Samuelson can spot a gold digger when he sees one. So when his ailing father announces his engagement to the private nurse he's only known for two months, Beckett has to step in. Before long he realizes he realizes she's the perfect next Mrs. Samuelson. If only he was the intended groom...

How Not to Mess with a Millionaire
a Mediterranean Millionaires novel by Regina Kyle

Interior decorator Zoe Ryan's life resembles a country song. What's a girl to do? Leave everything behind for a bit....in Italy. When she gets there, she finds a surprise—millionaire restaurateur Dante Sabbatini in the kitchen. In his underwear. Making coffee. It's suddenly not only hot outside ... but what is he doing inside, in her temporary kitchen? The very thing, it seems, that she's trying to avoid, and resisting is impossible.

Reforming the CEO
a South Beach novel by Marisa Cleveland

Reece Rowe's going to get a taste of what she's been missing and heads to hot Vincent Ferguson's office to find out what the women in South Beach already seem to know about him. CEO Vin Ferguson has to improve his image with his financial backers, and his friends suggest dating a respectable woman. Ridiculous. Because delectable but snooty socialites like Reece are out of his league. But he can't believe what she just proposed...

www.ingramcontent.com/pod-product-compliance
Lightning Source LLC
Chambersburg PA
CBHW020909180626
46816CB00007BA/2309